Crooks' Vendetta

by **Hamilton Teed**

(George Heber (Hamilton) Teed (1886-1938)

First Published by:

Columbine Publishing Company Ltd., London

1939

Stillwoods Edition 2018

Stillwoods.Blogspot.Ca
GHTeed.Blogspot.Ca

Catalogue Information:
Title: Crooks' Vendetta
Author: Hamilton Teed
(George Heber (Hamilton) Teed (1886-1938)
First Published: Columbine Publishing Company Ltd., London 1939 (presumed – may have been published serially in magazines.)
This Edition: Stillwoods, 2018.
ISBN Canada: 978-1-988304-55-7
Blog: Stillwoods.Blogspot.Ca and GHTeed.Blogspot.Ca
Storefront: http://www.lulu.com/spotlight/lulubook22

THRILLS, thrills, and again more thrills! As the writer of stirring, gripping tales of adventure, crime, detection, and quick-moving romance, Hamilton Teed needs no introduction to the reading public. In this, his latest novel, *Crooks' Vendetta,* Teed deals with the "snatch game," that foulest of all rackets—kidnapping. The story passes swiftly across the world. To call it breathless would be to do it an injustice. It moves too quickly. It is great stuff.

Hamilton Teed from New Brunswick, Canada, is known as a writer of thrillers as the summary above states. His prolific works were mostly published in England and in the form of 'pulps', magazines of low quality paper published for the reading public. The heroes in these magazines were either Nelson Lee or Sexton Blake; in hardback, due to copyright issues, those names never appear. Stillwoods has been unable to locate an original pulp version of this novel but it probably exists.
Doug Frizzle, September 2018.

CHAPTER I   BRADY ON HIS UPPERS

WHEN "Flash" Brady landed back in New York after a certain disastrous experience in the Latin-American republic of Costa Blanca, it was through no wish of his own that he and his beautiful partner, Gloria Ravissa, disembarked at that port.

They had no choice in the matter. In fact, they were extremely lucky to get away from the tropics at all. The only alternative was for Gloria Ravissa to remain south until opportunity offered for a passage to some other place, while Brady went on the beach.

And so few places were open to them. Indeed, there was a big risk in their attempting to land in New York, but, because they made the voyage in a small banana steamer that had accommodation for only eight passengers, they stepped through the barriers at New York with no more than a cursory glance.

Had the officials higher up known what a prize a junior had let past him, there would have been ructions for that young man.

With only a little over a hundred dollars between them, they hadn't much choice of where to go or what to do.

The first essential was to get under cover, and this is was not difficult for Brady to arrange, for he knew the city inside out, and was *persona grata* wherever crooks hang out.

He chose, as a temporary lodging, a small hotel on the east side, well down towards Water Street. Here he was in the midst of those whom the police gave a wide berth, was assured of the temporary protection of the big-shot gangster of that particular district, and was near enough to Broadway and the White-Light districts to reach them quickly enough for any business he might have the chance to turn.

Within two hours of the time when he and Gloria Ravissa walked into the shady hotel on East Houston Street, Brady was abroad again, making necessary contacts with the crooks of the district, and keeping eyes and ears open for a chance to turn something profitable.

Pug Legrand, the beer racketeer of the district, was pleasant enough to him. He offered Brady a job toting beer and spirits from his alky cooking factory to the speakeasies of the district, a job where a man goes out on a loaded dray with two or three typewriters— machine-guns—in case of a raid from federal authorities or hijackers.

Fifty dollars a run if the load came through without trouble; a hundred bucks a run if there was trouble and still the load came through.

If there was trouble and it didn't come through, then it didn't make any difference what price Pug Legrand offered, because you would never collect it, for the simple reason that you'd be as dead as mutton.

If things came to the worst, Brady would take such a job as a fill-in. Hence he stalled with Pug Legrand, thanking him, and promising to look him up.

But while that hundred odd dollars of his own lasted, Brady wasn't going out after small cheese like fifty dollars a run with such risk attached. It was Brady who preferred to sit in behind with the big shots while someone else worked for the small money. Still, beggars can't be choosers, and he knew he might come to it before he finished. Certainly working for Pug Legrand was better than being in quod.

He did not return to Gloria Ravissa that evening, but of all places he should choose to visit, with the whole of New York open, was Coney Island, that fantastic resort of New Yorkers down the bay, past Rockaway Beach.

Brady hadn't been near the place since the famous passage of Halley's Comet in 1910. He remembered it as a vast expanse of wooden boardwalk, flimsy houses where all sorts of sideshows and money-taking stunts were pulled, chop suey restaurants, switchback railways, dance-hall after dance-hall, and, in those days, a myriad saloons.

He found a place grown treble the size. But, all in all, it wasn't much different, except that the old-fashioned dance-music was screaming jazz, and while one could get a drink all right, it needed a little finesse to get inside.

It was not the sort of spot one would have thought a criminal adventurer like "Flash" Brady would choose for an inspiration.

As a matter of fact it was more some idle decision than anything else that took him there. It was a beautiful evening and crowded with people thousands upon thousands of New Yorkers trying to grab a drink of refreshing sea-breeze before returning to the stifling city.

Brady had absolutely nothing in view. While he walked about, pausing now and then like some country jay to watch a side-show, he kept a mechanical eye open for any chance that might turn up. But he'd have done that in the Waldorf-Astoria on Fifth Avenue, in the

Hotel Venetia in London, or, for the matter of that, in the Pope's palace in Vatican City.

And it was while he was idling about that, to his amazement, his eye fell on a couple whom he recognised, having met them when he was in New York the last time.

It was as surprising to see this pair at Coney Island as himself, or Brady would have thought so, did he not know that, on occasion, New Yorkers of all classes took a run down to Coney.

The woman was better known to him by feature than the man, for not so long before she had been fairly prominent on the New York stage, and had gained a certain notoriety for, firstly, having married a very rich man, and, secondly, having been divorced by him after a good deal of disgraceful conduct.

As Caroline Errol, wife of an Englishman who had made many, many millions in Wall Street, she could have occupied a stable position in New York society.

But that did not appeal to her, and when Mark Errol, her long-suffering husband, saw how things were, he made it easy enough for her to secure her freedom. It was said, too, that he had been very generous with her in the matter of settlements.

From that moment she had thrown off all pretence at respectability. She had boldly appeared with the sort of associates she preferred, and not long after the divorce she had married the man whom Brady saw her with on this night at Coney Island —one Darrell Richfield, a well-known New York gambler, "con" man, and crook generally.

He possessed the bold sort of handsomeness that appeals to a certain type of woman, and, as far as Brady knew, the pair had been hitting the high spots ever since their marriage.

His keen eye appraised them now as they walked on the wide broadwalk ahead of him. Here and there little points told him that things were probably not quite so prosperous with them as they might wish, and his quick, criminal mind was debating if there might be some way in which he could turn the circumstances to his own benefit when he almost paused as he saw Darrell Richfield perform as slick a feat of legerdemain as it had ever been his fortune to look upon.

The incident took place in front of an ornate erection called "The Palace of a Thousand Beauties." Above the gilt and mirrors was painted a string of pictures of young women in as near the nude as the law would permit to be exhibited.

On a platform under this a man was shouting himself hoarse, inveigling people to mount the steps to the box-office, assuring them that every girl in the show had at one time or another been a member of the Ziegfeld Follies.

As every chorus-girl in New York makes the same claim, that didn't mean anything to one as sophisticated as Brady. But it evidently carried weight with the out-of-town people who listened, for at the rate the men were mounting the steps it looked as if business was brisk.

It was here, then, that the incident took place which roused Brady's unstinted admiration.

Just in front of Darrell Richfield and his wife was an elderly man dressed in prosperous grey, and, from the whole stamp of him, undoubtedly a well-off country business man visiting the city.

It was plain that he was duly impressed by the spiel of the barker up above, and was anxious to enter the place, being held back by a certain amount of shyness.

That, however, he would soon overcome when other men started to go up, and here it was that Darrell Richfield pulled his stunt. At one moment he was a yard away from the man. At the next he was hovering close to him for no more than a second or two, and at the next he and his wife were sauntering on once more, the only difference in conditions being that now Richfield had possession of a very fat wallet which, in his legerdemain, he had abstracted from the old fellow's hip pocket.

Brady followed them with interest. He didn't know how much money there might be in that wallet, but he thought the chances were it would contain a pretty good wad, and before he finished he intended that half should be transferred from Richfield to himself.

Once he almost lost his quarry, and as they proceeded farther he saw that they were working gradually towards the exit. No doubt by now the out-of-town business man had discovered his loss and was making a row with the police. But it would be hopeless to find the culprit among those packed thousands, and, indeed, the police on duty at Coney would have thought there was something radically wrong if they didn't get about two score complaints every night of pocket-picking.

Brady thought it would be a good idea to make his approach

before the pair got away from Coney. He wanted to have them within call of the Coney police in order to run his bluff.

So he quickened his step and touched Richfield lightly on the shoulder. The "con" man flung round as if a bomb had exploded under him.

At sight of Brady's grinning countenance a look of intense relief appeared on his face.

"Oh, it's you!" he said, with a swift return to his usual suavity. "Fancy seeing you down in this dump! How are you? I thought you were out of the city. You've met the wife, I think."

Brady shook hands and bowed gallantly to the woman who had thrown away security and millions for—this.

He replied to or evaded Richfield's questions as he thought best, and then, when they would have taken him along with them towards the exit, he laid a restraining hand on Richfield's arm.

"I say, don't go just yet," he begged good-humouredly. "Have mercy on the returned prodigal and take me where I can get a drink. I'm as dry as the Sahara, and you know all the ropes."

"Why—er—sure!" agreed Richfield. "Do you mind, Carrie?"

"I could drink a pailful myself," she said throatily.

So they turned, and piloted by the knowing Richfield, wormed their way through the crowd until they came to a building in front of which was a restaurant.

But Richfield turned into a very narrow passage at one side, and after a good deal of dodging under side-shows and actually stooping under one section of a switchback railway, brought them to a closed door in a very shadowy spot.

He knocked here, and a tiny wicket suddenly opened. The man inside evidently knew him well, for the door was opened immediately after, and the trio stepped into a small dingy hall.

From here they were taken into a small room furnished only with a table and some chairs.

The man who had admitted them, a hard-featured man with one side of his face twisted through a great scar, made his demands as well as the mutilation of his cheek-muscles and a chew of gum would permit.

"Whachawant, Rich?"

"Got some decent whisky?"

"It's the doos, I'm tellin' you."

5

"Shoot us a bottle, then. How much?"

"Twenty-five bucks."

Richfield was about to pay, but with an airy gesture Brady took out the roll that represented all he possessed in the world. From this he peeled thirty dollars.

"A five spot for yourself, bo."

The one with the scar grabbed the notes, kissed them, and stuffed them into his trousers' pocket. Then he vanished, but he was back in a few minutes with a bottle of whisky purporting to be the distilling of a well-known British firm, three glasses, and a bottle of water.

He disappeared once more, closing the door after him. Brady motioned for Richfield to pour the stuff, and it was when the other half rose, leaning towards him to reach his glass, that Brady shot out his hand and drew forth the thick wallet that Richfield had separated from its proper owner.

Richfield dropped the bottle with an oath. Brady flashed the wallet out of sight, rescued the bottle, and had his automatic across the table in a series of movements so quick as to dazzle one.

"All right, Rich," he said softly. "Sit down, laddie. Don't get excited. I saw you lift this, and it feels like a good one. We're going to share."

The woman's eyes were murderous, but they also held fear, for she knew something of "Flash" Brady's character, and she knew his gun threat was no empty one.

Richfield was sitting, still cursing, when she laid a hand on his arm.

"Wait, Darrell. Don't have trouble here."

"What do you mean by pulling a thing like that?" he demanded. "You're a devil of a pal, you are! We bring you in here for a snifter, and you throw a hold-up!"

"Keep your shirt on, Rich," returned Brady coolly. "If there isn't much in here you can have the lot. But if the wad is as good as it feels, we're going fifty-fifty. I'm needing money just as badly as you seem to need it. Or were you just keeping your hand in? If so perhaps I'd better hang on to the lot."

"I tell you we need that haul!" snarled Richfield.

"Then we're in the same box. Keep cool and let's see what we've got."

He laid the pistol close to his right hand and opened the wallet. It was of well-worn calfskin with a silver monogram on the outside, but the lettering was so rubbed with long years of use that it was impossible to decipher it.

Brady's eyes lit up, and both the Richfields gave a gasp as he dumped out from one side of the wallet a thick fold of yellowback notes and from the other an almost equally thick fold of greenbacks.

There were some letters and other papers as well, but Brady ignored these for the moment, pushed the wallet aside and, with a warning glance at the pair opposite, began to count the yellowbacks.

"Six thousand eight hundred dollars," he announced when he had finished. "That means three thousand four hundred each of that lot."

"Look here," burst out Richfield, "if we've got to submit to this hold-up, then the division should be thirds. Carrie is entitled to a full share."

Brady's fingers caressed the blued steel of the automatic.

"You two are married, aren't you?" he asked suavely.

"Of course we are. But what has that to do with it?"

"Well, then, if you are married, you must be one. Married folk are always counted that way. So you get one share—that is half. I am being perfectly fair."

His teeth showed in a grin about as attractive as that of a hungry hyena, and he went on counting the greenbacks.

"Only six hundred odd in this lot," he announced. "I'll take three hundred, and you can have the rest. There you are, Rich, and count yourself darned lucky! We both need the stuff, and we've got a nice little egg to go on with. Don't grouse. Now let's have that drink."

Richfield apparently accepted the situation, for he pocketed his share of the money, and watched while Brady went through the other contents of the wallet.

There was nothing here of any use to them, however, and when Richfield was satisfied of this, Brady pushed the wallet in his pocket, remarking as he did so:

"There's a card in there showing the hotel where the old boy is staying. He'll need those business papers. I'll post the wallet to him. After all, he deserves to have those back after financing us as he has. But what a darned old fool to come down to a place like Coney Island with a wad like that in his hip pocket!"

The Richfields agreed and, indeed, as the drinking progressed the little trouble that had threatened was quite forgotten. Indeed, by the time they had punished a second bottle of whisky they were the best of friends once more, and so much so that the pair confided in Brady a matter which had been exercising their minds for some time past.

It was an affair which they planned to work upon Mrs. Richfield's former husband, the multi-millionaire, Mark Errol, but, up to now, they either lacked the nerve or the ingenuity to bring it to a head.

The figure they had set themselves was a hundred thousand dollars. But before they parted company that night Brady was in the thing up to his neck.

"A hundred grand!" he scoffed. "Chicken feed! If you've got a thing like that on Mark Errol it's worth the best part of a million, and I don't mean dollars! I mean pounds sterling!"

CHAPTER II   THE FIRST COUP

DESPITE the temptation to make whoopee on the six hundred odd pounds he had dragged down so easily that evening, Brady got down to business.

He knew enough about the man they intended to rook to realise that there, if it were worked properly, was one of the fattest things that had ever come his way.

But it would need very careful planning. It wasn't a thing to be rushed. Their intended victim had been shrewd enough to walk into Wall Street and take out many millions from under the noses of the hard-bitten habitues of the Street. Therefore, he was not the one to fall for any half-baked scheme.

Moreover, he had now retired from Wall Street and had left the United States to return to his own country. Whatever was pulled must be done in England, and Brady needed no telling that the *modus operandi* must needs be of a very different character from what might be adopted in America.

What appealed to him, however, was the fact that they possessed a card which, with ordinary men, would prove a strong lever. With the man they had in prospect it all depended on his individual character how much of that quality known as father love he possessed.

For the "nigger in the woodpile" was the existence of a child, a boy, about which Mark Errol was entirely ignorant.

Brady did not bother himself trying to understand Carrie Richfield's reasons for suppressing this important event from her husband, as Errol had been at the time.

Gloria Ravissa could guess the odd twist in a woman's mind that would send her off in secret to bear her child, and then, out of some perversity born of hatred or other more obscure emotion, conceal the fact from the person who had the most right to know.

Before proceeding with an elaboration of the scheme, Brady took pains to satisfy himself that everything was jake, as the saying goes.

He knew that if there were the slightest flaw in the claim, they would never land a man like Errol. Nor did he intend to get mixed up in anything so crude as the Lindbergh affair. The whole country was still seething over that.

But when he had finished checking up on the evidence submitted by the Richfields, he knew that the case was solid riveted and

9

absolutely water-tight.

Flighty, unstable, foolish she might have been, but in this one thing Carrie Richfield had been completely efficient. Every proof that was needed was available to Brady, and when he had reached that point, he set his fertile criminal mind to devise a means of separating Mark Errol from anything up to a million sterling.

He would have none of the haphazard plan on which the Richfields had been working when he ran into them that night at Coney Island. Better, far better, had it been for them had Brady never come into it, for from the moment he took control their chances of cashing in were to grow smaller and smaller, and, as for the woman, a very different result than she looked forward to was in waiting.

One thing that tended to put complete control into the hands of Brady and Gloria Ravissa was the fact that both the Richfields were entirely ignorant of England and of social and criminal procedure there.

This forced them to depend on whatever Brady said, and certainly it could not be said that he lacked experience in most ways of that tight little island.

But something far deeper than the original plan began to work in the mind of the master criminal.

The only person who knew about that, however, was Gloria Ravissa, and even she only learned what Brady was aiming at. Not until he advanced much further with his plans would he know whether he could bring it off or not.

If he did, it would be one of the worst double-crosses ever recorded in criminal history. If it failed, it would not affect the original scheme.

"Why should the Richfields sit in on this thing, anyway?" he had said to Gloria Ravissa when discussing the matter.

"Well, after all, they proposed it, and we are using her child," rejoined the girl.

Brady shrugged.

"What difference does that make? We're all on the make, aren't we? Look at Richfield. For years now he has been living by his wits. He's deep in the confidence game—a tin-horn sport crook, I call him. And take the woman. She had everything a dame could wish for. And what did she do with it? She chucked it all away for that four-flusher. They don't deserve to cash in on a rich plum like this."

"How will you keep them out of it?"

"You leave it to me. I'll figure a way."

"But if you take the Richfields to England, you'll have them on your hands."

Brady looked at her oddly.

"Listen, my dear. When I have found it convenient to get rid of anyone who becomes an incubus, I usually succeed, don't I?"

Gloria Ravissa shrugged. She knew better than to argue with him.

"And after?" she asked after a pause. "We can't come back here, and England will be too hot for us. Where will we go?"

"Now you've asked something I can answer. You know about my old friend Count Larida."

"The Spaniard?"

"Well, call him a Spaniard if you wish, but he wouldn't thank you. He is very touchy on the point of race. He is a Catalonian, and lets you know it. You've read of the trouble they've been having lately in Barcelona."

"Of course."

"Well, Count Larida is up to the neck in that. And it looks as if he and his crowd were going to pull off the independence they are after. The Spanish Government can do little. Larida and I were good friends when I was with Abdel Krim in the Riff. He wouldn't be a bit sorry to see me if I landed in Barcelona with a wad of money in my jeans. And Larida would ask no questions. He would want a slice, of course. That would be all right. In return he'd see that no extradition measures would be taken even if we were traced. That is what is in my mind as a getaway after we finish in England. At any rate, I'll get in touch with Larida and see how he feels. As I told you before, I'll figure a way out of all these things."

He did, though before the game was played out, cold, stark murder was to enter the lists.

It soon became evident to Brady that a good deal of spade-work would need to be done in England before the thing could be sprung on the intended victim.

Up to now he had drawn freely on the money he had got that night at Coney Island as well as the Richfields' share.

It would need considerably more to take him to England and keep him financed there until he figured out the best way of approach. Brady was a free spender, and he knew that, keeping under cover as would be necessary in England, he would have to spend heavily.

Moreover, there was always the unknown factor, and if the plot was going to stand up, then he must be prepared to put up capital on immediate call.

So despite the fact that he was intending to double-cross his accomplices, he set to work with Darrell Richfield, and for a couple of weeks or so the main plan had to be shelved while they scouted round New York for money.

Legrand, the big shot in the booze and dope racket, had nothing to offer except what he had first told Brady he could have. But that provided no more than chicken-feed, to use Brady's contemptuous phrase. What he needed was to get up against the big money.

"I've got to have something else, Legrand," he pressed. "You know me all right, and you know that I run with the big fellows. I've got a big thing on over in England, but it is going to need capital. If you will see me through this, give me a chance to drag down a few grand, I'll turn the trick your way some day."

The gangster, sitting in the back room of one ot the thousand-odd speakeasies he controlled, shifted his cigar and grinned crookedly.

"You can't do anything for me, fella. But no one can say that I ever let one of the gang down. I'll pass along the word and see what I can do for you. Come and see me again to-night."

Brady was back in that same room at ten o'clock the same night. He waited there until two o'clock in the morning before Legrand showed up.

"Well, fella," he greeted Brady, "I've got something for you. But it's going to take nerve, big boy. Have you got plenty?"

"You try me!" grunted Brady.

"Then listen! You know how the different New York banks transfer their money to the Federal Reserve Bank each day?"

"Not exactly. I know that they use armoured cars."

"I'm telling you. Every morning a bunch of armoured cars go out and call at the different banks. A uniformed messenger goes into the banks, where the money is all ready. It is handed over to him, he takes the bag and dumps it into the car, and that's all. The armoured car carries two armed guards and some of them a typewriter. Got that?"

"Yes."

"Well, big boy, that's where you come in. Now, this transfer is in the hands of a single authorised trucking company. They have a regular schedule. Everything snaps right to the minute. That's where you come in."

"As how?"

"I've fixed it all up for you. To-morrow morning at one minute to eleven—no sooner, no later—you walk into the Merchant's Trust and Discount Bank in East Sixteenth Street. You go straight to the counter at the far end on the left. You say you have come for the money for the Federal Reserve, and see what happens. If you get the stuff, you beat it quick. Around the corner in Broadway you'll find a closed green car waiting for you. If you don't get the money, you beat it anyway, because at eleven sharp the regular guy will be in there asking for the money."

"But how will he hand it over to me?"

"Because, fella, you're going to be wearing a uniform of that authorised trucking company. We're working on psychology, fella. We're counting on that guy behind the counter coming across mechanically as he has come across thousands of times before. If he does glance at the clock, it'll be so near the mark as to make no difference. You'll have less than a minute to pull it off. But there it is, if you want it."

"What do I get out of it?"

"One-third, and a big chunk it is."

"I'll take you on, Legrand. And I'll pull it off if that bird pushes the stuff across the counter."

Brady knew the risk of failure. He knew that even if he did get the money, he stood every chance of walking right into the arms of the authorised messenger as he left the bank; and that would mean a long term in prison without any hanky-panky, for the United States federal authorities don't stand for any monkeying with their banking affairs.

It would mean, too, risking the whole thing he had been working on, but he saw no other way of getting the necessary capital, and he was always ready to take a gamble on any odds.

That night he reconnoitred the neighbourhood of the bank which was to be victimised. He got the whole layout clearly in his mind, even to counting the number of steps leading to the lobby, and estimating the distance from the lobby to the kerb. Then, walking slowly, he paced the distance from the door to the kerb in Broadway where the closed green car was to be waiting.

He figured the results, and told himself that, if there was no delay inside the bank, the thing could be pulled off and the green car reached just about in the minute he would have at his disposal. Any delay, no matter how brief, would imperil his chances. But that did not lessen his determination to have a shot at it.

At precisely two minutes to eleven the following morning Brady clad in the grey uniform of a messenger of the United States Trucking Corporation, stepped out of a taxi at the corner of East Sixteenth Street. Out of the corner of his eye he saw a closed green car just drawing into the kerb.

He walked along at a calculated pace, based on his investigations of the night before, so that it was exactly one minute to eleven when he entered the lobby of the bank.

He quickened his pace now, striding straight along towards the far end of the long counter on the left.

Here a bespectacled clerk was busy over a ledger. Brady tapped the counter lightly, and in a brisk voice said:

"I've come for the Federal Reserve money."

The clerk glanced up, saw the usual uniform, took a swift look at the clock, where the minute hand was, at that angle, practically on the hour, and mechanically took a leather bag from a shelf under the counter.

He pushed this across to Brady, whose fingers closed on it. He muttered his thanks, and, turning, started for the door.

He did not hasten. He knew almost to a second how much time he would have unless the authorised messenger should enter a trifle ahead of time.

No one accosted him as he passed out to the street.

Behind him, just turning into East Sixteenth Street, was the armoured car.

But Brady did not even see it. He covered the distance to Broadway just as he had paced it the night before, and then, as he reached the kerb, the door of the green saloon opened to engulf him.

The car drew away immediately. Brady leaned back behind drawn curtains that hid his uniform.

Half an hour later he laid the bag of money in front of Legrand.

"There's the jack," he said curtly.

The Big Shot smiled his twisted smile, and cut the leather round the lock. Then he dumped the contents on to the table, and when the total was made Brady found that he had walked away with one hundred and twenty thousand six hundred dollars.

One-third of that meant forty thousand two hundred dollars, or, say, ten thousand pounds at the present level of exchange. It was, he figured, more than enough for his purpose.

Two days later he sailed for England to arrange the preliminaries of the coup he was planning against the multi-millionaire, Mark Errol.

Gloria Ravissa remained in New York for the present. With her there the Richfields would not get out of hand.

CHAPTER III   MARK ERROL

GRANT RUSHTON'S first meeting with Mark Errol was at Hanworth.

He and Tony Fairways had gone out to the aerodrome to try out a new Puss Moth which Rushton had given to the lad to replace another which had suffered irreparable damage when crashing some time previously. It was not Tony who was flying the machine at the time, but a friend to whom he had lent it—a lucky young novice who had escaped practically unscathed.

Mark Errol was a very rich man.

He had returned to England about a year previously after a continued absence of some six years. In that year he had achieved a certain amount of unsought publicity owing to some spectacular flights he had made in his specially constructed Fairy Hat—the sort of flights that meant breakfast in London, lunch in Rome, tea in Paris, and dinner back in London.

He had also come into no little prominence through the masterly driving of his English racing car at Brooklands, Le Mans, and in Ireland.

He would have been on the front page of the papers far more often had Society and the reporters had their way. But Mark Errol was about as adroit in side-stepping their attentions as he was in handling 'plane and car, with the result that no one seemed to yet very close to him as a man.

There were, of course, all sorts of yarns about as to how he had gained his great wealth. It was said that he had gambled in wheat in the Argentine that he had sold enormous quantities of coffee in Brazil before the terrific slump in that commodity, that he had smuggled arms for the Chinese, that he had had the handling of a vast quantity of jewels belonging to the former Russian Royal Family.

Every yarn was wrong, not even approaching the facts. The truth was that Mark Errol was one of the few Englishmen who had ever gone into Wall Street and met the American stock operators on their own ground with great profit to himself.

For the first four years of his stay in New York he had been always riding high on the great bull market that lifted American stocks and shares to unheard of heights.

In 1929, just before the first gigantic slump hit Wall Street, Mark

Errol heard the faint rumbling of the coming earthquake. He got out of all his holdings at top prices of the market, was completely clear before that fatal October 29th.

And the same prescience told him that the first crash of the upheaval was but a forerunner of what was to come.

He sold short, and continued selling against the temporary rallies which were engineered by big operators to sustain the market and stop the threatening panic.

It is now known that nothing could stop the greatest slump in all history. Millions, billions in values disappeared as if they had possessed no more substance than mist. Prices tobogganed down and down until all humanity was staggering under the repeated blows. And during all this time Mark Errol was making millions of dollars that other people were losing.

A year before his return to England he had had enough. He sold out with no more emotion than he had watched prices tumbling in a wild chaos. And, with his enormous wealth in what he believed were the most stable investments left in a wondering and crazy world— British Government Bonds—he had come back to his own country.

Certain British Government officials knew of his vast holdings in Government stock; many bankers and Grant Rushton knew the truth. But none of them disillusioned the romance-building reporters or the sensation-loving public.

Grant Rushton's knowledge had come to him through his New York agent, Bryant Kennedy, who had had certain business transactions with Mark Errol in the States, knew of his dealings, and passed the information on to Rushton when Errol started for England.

Therefore Rushton was mildly interested to meet the man who had achieved such enormous success in six short years. Yet it was not through any financial or professional matter they met. It was through Tony who, on the occasion in question, got into conversation with Errol outside one of the hangars.

Errol had approached Rushton's assistant while he was making a preliminary survey of the Puss Moth.

"They tell me you are Tony, the young detective," he said, with a smile.

Tony grinned back cheerfully. One might have expected to find Mark Errol a big man of severe presence. He was nothing of the sort. Just about middle height, he was extraordinarily compact of build, and extremely well-proportioned. His skin was tanned deeply, for he was strictly an out-of-door man. His hair was fair and crisp, his eyes a very pleasant blue. In age he looked just what he was—about thirty-five.

"That's not quite right, sir," was Tony's response. "I am assistant to Mr. Grant Rushton."

"It's all the same, judging from what the papers say. And I've heard Bryant Kennedy in New York mention both you and Mr. Grant Rushton. My name is Errol—Mark Errol."

"I know that, sir. I've known you by sight for some time. That was a nifty bit of work you did at Le Mans last month in your B. G."

"Not so good, not so good. I'd like to meet Mr. Rushton. Does he ever come out here?"

"He's here now, Mr. Errol. That's the chief over there in the light-grey flannel suit. I fancy he'd be pleased to meet you as well. If you care to come along I'll introduce you."

"By all means."

That was how the two men first met, and so congenial did they find each other that they had frequent meetings afterwards.

Errol, who was very keen on criminology in an amateurish way, got into the habit of dropping in at Rushton's house in Jermyn Street, where he would yarn away about past cases of Rushton's until he would suddenly remember that he was probably keeping the famous detective from his work.

And on one or two occasions he went along with Rushton and Tony when they were engaged on a new case, as tickled as any schoolboy at being included.

Not that he inflicted—as he put it—himself on Rushton without some return. On the contrary, he was always at him and Tony to come down and stay with him at the place he had bought some six miles out of Henley and some two miles from Hambleden Lock.

They had done so on one occasion in the early summer of that year, and it was a matter of regret to Rushton that he had to return to London when he did, for with some two miles of excellent dry fly fishing in the stream that ran through the property, he was in his element.

It was a lovely old Georgian house that Errol had bought, and with something over three hundred acres of rich land, with the stream and a string of three private lakes, with beautiful old oaks and elms and noble beeches making the place more of a park than anything else, it was as attractive a property as one could find in all the Chilterns, and that means something even in England.

But this particular summer Rushton was very busy, and had been forced to postpone again and again his promise to go down for another week.

He had no idea then that, when he did go down next to Fingest Grange, it would be to plunge into one of the most baffling and dangerous cases he had ever tackled.

It came about thus:

One lovely warm day in July Mark Errol arrived at Jermyn Street in the black torpedo sports car which he usually preferred when driving himself. He had a choice among five cars, but all but two of those were strictly used for racing events.

He found Rushton and Tony employed with the morning mail, and begging them to carry on, he took down a volume of the famous "Index" in which Tony kept clippings of all the most important cases, and proceeded to lose himself among the fascinating entries.

It was only when Rushton finished dictating and lit his pipe that Errol took this as a sign that he was at liberty for the time being.

"I want you and Tony to come down for the week-end," he said abruptly. "Now, don't say 'no,'" he hastened to add, as he saw Rushton begin to smile deprecatingly. "This is something special, and, while I don't want to go into matters now, I will say that I am asking you professionally."

"You don't mean you have a case for me," said Rushton incredulously.

"Not exactly a case. But I want your advice, and, if you will give it, your help. But I want you down there before I go into matters. We won't talk about fees and all that sort of thing. We'll settle that later. But this is strictly business with the proviso that you come as my guests, too. I was thinking that Tony could fly you down in his machine. I'd like to see what you think of my private landing-ground. This is only Friday morning, so you've got the whole day to dispose of urgent business matters and leave this afternoon. I'll expect you both before dinner, so don't disappoint me."

He was already on his feet with his motoring cap and gauntlets in his hand. Rushton smiled, and was trying to protest; but Errol would not listen. He was out through the door while Rushton was still talking, and then followed the determined closing of the front door.

Tony grinned at Rushton.

"And that's that, chief. He doesn't intend to take 'no' for an answer."

"I'd like to go all right, old son; but there is that Pilcher matter."

"I've got the papers all ready. If you can get hold of Mrs. Pilcher during the afternoon we could manage it okay. It won't take me long to polish off these letters and other routine. I can have everything ready for your signature by three o'clock, and we could leave Hanworth between four and five. It's a peach of a day for flying."

Rushton gave in with a smile.

"Okay, as you say. We'll go. You seem to have made up your mind."

"Well," confessed Tony, "Mr. Errol has been telling me so much about that private landing-ground of his that I'd like to see it. You remember it was only lined out when we were down there."

"And I might do a little worming for trout in clear water," murmured Rushton absently. "They wouldn't look at a fly under these conditions."

"I wonder if he was only kidding about having a case," said Tony as he pulled the typewriter towards him.

"I'm not so sure. Once or twice I thought Errol was on the point of broaching some subject of a very private nature, but he always sheered off. Maybe something has been bothering him for some time, and now has come to a head so that he must deal with it."

"Well, you never can tell where a pimple may start," rejoined Tony flippantly.

It was just half-past four when they garaged the Grey Panther at Hanworth and climbed into Tony's two-seater Puss Moth.

It was still lacking a minute or so to a quarter-past five when Tony picked up the white-painted outlines of Errol's private landing-ground after getting his bearings from the old Saxon church tower at Fingest.

Errol, with his two chauffeur mechanics, who also looked after his Fairy Bat, was on the ground to meet them.

Tony made a sweet landing and taxied to a stop not a yard from where the little group waited. Then he and Rushton tumbled out, and, walking through a yew-lined path that took them along the side of a sunken Italian garden, they came out on to a small lawn that was almost entirely enclosed with high, smoothly clipped hedges. They knew the place for their host's private retreat.

He waved his hand towards a table that had been set in a small arbour at one end.

"Tea is ready. You know your way to the cloakroom off the hall. Get out of your flying togs and come along."

They obeyed while Errol lit a cigarette and paced up and down. Seeing him now, when he believed himself unobserved, Grant Rushton would have realised that it was no trivial matter on which he desired his advice.

The smooth, ironed-out mask of the cool stock operator was gone. The enigmatical narrowing of the eyes of the racing motorist had disappeared.

Instead there appeared a countenance that was clouded—nay, haggard with worry. The eyes, usually so steady, shot this way and that in nervous jerks. The mouth was drawn as if some muscular support had suddenly refused to function. Mark Errol looked, in that moment, more like sixty-five than thirty-five.

A glimpse of white through the opening in the hedge caused his features to undergo a remarkable metamorphosis. By the time a short, white-jacketed Japanese servant appeared with a loaded tray Mark Errol appeared as usual, though when he had set the tray down the little Jap shot him a swift look as if he knew what deep-seated anxiety was racking his master.

"You will wait and serve, Mitsu."

"Very good, master."

The Jap moved back and stood unobtrusively, his flat Oriental eyes fixed on the ground.

Yet he knew something of his master's trouble, for he was the only living being that was, so far, in Mark Errol's confidence. He had been Errol's personal servant when he first went to New York, he had remained with him during the six years there, and he had come to England with him when Errol returned to the land of his fathers.

"Mr. Rushton and Mr. Tony have gone to the cloak-room?"

"Yes, master."

"Liddle and Stevens are bringing their bags up from the landing-ground. You will see to them, Mitsu."

"Yes, master. Their rooms are ready."

"Good. Nothing else has come, Mitsu?"

The Jap took a quick look at his master.

"Nothing, master."

"Liddle is taking the limousine to meet them. You have told Mrs. Dean to hold back dinner until they come?"

"Yes, master, everything is seen to."

"Good boy. I think Mr. Rushton and Mr. Tony are coming now."

He was right. Rushton and Tony swung in through the opening a moment or two later, and with a friendly nod to Mitsu, whom they had seen before on their previous visit, they sat down.

No one would have dreamed to peep into that delightful, shady retreat that anxiety hung heavy upon one of the trio at the table, and that grim tragedy hovered close at hand.

No man could have appeared more the favourite of fortune, the adored of Lady Luck than Mark Errol. Possessed of millions, even in sterling, still on the sunny side of forty, with perfect health and an abounding vigour for the cleanest type of life, one of the most perfect little estates in all England, a personal servant who was perfection, discretion and loyalty personified, other servants who ordered his life like a well-oiled machine and the means to gratify every whim—all that, and a nifty little private yacht lying at Southampton to boot—and one would have thought he simply must be happy.

Yet why that brief discarding of the mask when he was alone? Why that surreptitious glance which the devoted Mitsu gave him when he thought himself unobserved?

It is said that everyone has a skeleton in his cupboard. If that is so, then Mark Errol's was beginning to rattle ominously.

But Grant Rushton got a sudden glimpse into the shadows when, after Mitsu had withdrawn, Errol turned and said quietly:

"I got you down here upon a very special matter, Rushton. I don't know yet how grave it is going to prove, but I shall have an idea before the night is over. I want you to know the facts before some other people arrive, so I am going to give you my confidence, and, of course, that includes Tony. May I go ahead?"

"Please do," was Rushton's equally quiet response.

CHAPTER IV   THE SHADOW

"I MUST go back to my early days in New York," said Errol after he had lit a cigarette. "This business really begins with my marriage."

Tony could scarce refrain from a quick glance, but Rushton gave no sign, though this was the first either of them had heard that Mark Errol had been married. Certainly no household could be more of a bachelor establishment than Fingest Grange.

"You did not know that, of course," he added.

"No."

"Your New York man, Bryant Kennedy, knows."

"He would not tell me unless I were to act officially in some way. He did tell me that you were returning to England, but that is all."

"He is dependable—very. To proceed. I married shortly after I arrived in New York. I was divorced three years ago."

"I guessed that."

"Yes. My wife—that was—was an actress of considerable ability—off the stage as well as on."

Rushton made no comment upon this subtle irony.

"She was born in the Middle West, and was a winner of a beauty prize when those ridiculous competitions first became popular. She got a place in a popular beauty chorus and she married from there—not me."

"She was divorced when you met her?"

"She had been divorced twice. When I met her she was playing on the legitimate stage on Broadway. She was leading woman in the hit of the season, and, as I said, possessed great ability. We were married two months after I met her. The understanding was that she was to give up the stage, but after six months she began to grow restless, and difficulties of temperament caused increasing friction between us."

"That is easily understood."

"At last, to keep the peace, I consented that she should return to the stage. I was also fool enough to finance the production. I was both husband and what the Americans call a 'sugar daddy.' Well, the play was a flop, a very bad flop. She became more difficult than ever to handle. I financed two more plays, both flops. Then I came home one night to find that she had flown the coop."

"Back to the stage again?"

"Yes. She had joined a stock company through the Middle West. It had been organised by the fellow who had been leading man in the plays I financed. I guess he was a pretty decent sort of guy, for she left him flat on the road and made for Hollywood. He never squealed to me. She thought that all she had to do in Hollywood was to announce who she was, and the big shots in the film world would break a leg trying to reach her first. She was mistaken. I had to send her money to get back to New York. She was quiet enough for a few months; but then she faded away again, and I decided to cut the string. That is where I employed Bryant Kennedy. He used to talk a lot about you. He found out my wife was running with a queer bunch of night birds. Then I went to Reno and got a divorce. I had Kennedy draw up a settlement. I allowed no alimony, but I made her a flat gift of one hundred thousand dollars. She signed an agreement absolving me from all further claim."

"I should say you were generous."

"It was enough, but I didn't begrudge it. If she'd known how much I was really worth even then she'd have put up a big holler for five times that sum. She was the worst gold-digger I have ever seen. But I won't crab her. I was a mug and a fool, and I paid. Well, she married again—a fellow of the name of Richfield, Darrell Richfield. Ever heard the name?"

"I don't think so."

"Kennedy knows about him. Kennedy tells me he is a flash crook and gambler, confidence man, blackmailer—anything like that. She was running with him before I divorced her."

"I see. I suppose he got his fingers on the hundred thousand."

"They were greasy fingers. The hundred thousand didn't last them long. And now for the meat of the whole thing. I've kept this until the last because it will explain why certain people are coming here to-night, and why I want your aid."

He lit a fresh cigarette, passing his case to Rushton. Rushton shook his head and kept on at his pipe.

"She fooled me all along the line," went on Errol. "If you had heard from Kennedy about what he was doing for me he would have told you that he was searching for a child. But he did not have my permission to do so."

"He never hinted at such a thing."

"He wouldn't. This is what happened. When I had been married

24

about five months my wife told me that she would have to go to her old home in Illinois where her mother was dangerously ill. I thought this rather a daughterly desire, so I made no difficulty. In fact, I did everything in my power to help, and told her to get the best doctors in Chicago if necessary. The months passed. It was more than four months before she returned, and when she did she told me her mother had died. As a matter of fact, the mother had been dead for several years; also her father. What happened was the secret birth of my son. I can't tell you why she suppressed all knowledge from me unless even then she hated me, as she confessed later, and was planning to have something with which to make me suffer later on."

"It seems unnatural."

"It was unnatural. You wonder how I discovered the truth. I only knew it about six months ago. I received a letter from a girl who had been my wife's personal maid. She had been with my wife at the time and had been bribed to keep secrecy. Then there was a row, and she was dismissed. I suppose my ex-wife thought that, being in England, I was safe. Well, I got in touch with Bryant Kennedy at once. I told him to get hold of that girl and locate the child. He did so."

"He is very dependable, as I said."

"And again—yes. Then what do you think I told him to do?"

"Get hold of the child?"

"Not exactly. I told him to put a watch on the boy and not let him be spirited away. He was in the care of a woman in a small village in Illinois. Then I had him get in touch with my ex-wife, who is, of course, now Mrs. Richfield. I authorised him to offer her another hundred thousand dollars for surrender of the child and all papers she might have pertaining to it. She refused, as I expected. I got Kennedy on the trans-Atlantic telephone, and told him to offer up to five hundred thousand dollars cash."

"A hundred thousand pounds. And she refused?"

"She did. That was enough. Kennedy had further instructions from me, and he carried them out."

"You mean he got hold of the boy?

"He did. He was placed secretly in a very good home for children. And there he remained until about two weeks ago."

"Ah! And then?"

"There must have been a leakage somewhere. They found out the place and kidnapped him back. Here is Kennedy's cablegram."

He took from his pocket an envelope, extracted a slip of paper and handed it to Rushton. The detective read:

"Mark Errol,

"Fingest Grange,

"Fingest, Bucks, England.

"Profoundly regret inform you child taken from home by force. Am employing every means to locate. Cannot yet find any trace of Richfields. Will keep you posted.

"(Signed) KENNEDY.

"And since?" asked Rushton as he handed it back.

"Nothing but a daily telephone conversation with Kennedy. He can discover nothing. It seems that a force of gunmen shot up the staff at the home where the boy was living. They collared him and made off in a fast car—no one knows where. But, of course, my ex-wife and her present husband are behind it. You know there are thousands of kidnapping cases in the States, Rushton, that never receive publicity. The parents are too fearful that the children will receive harm to go to the police. So they pay the ransom. That is the line I took. I have told Kennedy to offer anything if he can get the baby back. But he can't find the Richfields."

"It looks as though they may be making you sweat in order to demand a very high ransom."

"If that was all, I'd possess myself with patience and wait until they showed their hand. I don't blame my ex-wife so much as Richfield. He is an out-and-out crook; she has only gone astray through folly, and I guess must have got deeply into his power. But they have shown their hands—only to-day."

"It is they whom you expect this evening."

"You have guessed it exactly. They are due to arrive just before dinner. I had a telephone message early this morning from my ex-wife. She spoke from London. I told them to come down as they suggested, but not to arrive before this evening. I wanted to see you first. Now you know the whole thing. I suppose they are coming to make some colossal demand upon me. Between you and me, I will pay anything to get my boy back. But they will not accept a fair sum. I am sure of that. Richfield has found out in some way that I am worth far more than they ever dreamed. Well, it would hurt like the devil to see that crook get away with too much of my money as well as my wife.

"And I don't blame you," said Rushton warmly. "You offered half a million dollars—a hundred thousand pounds. It was more than enough. They must intend to demand millions."

"That is my belief."

"Naturally I shall do what I can, Errol. But you know this is blackmail in this country, and blackmail is regarded as a very serious crime. If they intend staying in your house and make no bones about their demands and conditions, it should not be difficult to lay a police-trap and then charge them with blackmail. Why don't you let me send for my friend, Chief Inspector Thomas of Scotland Yard."

"That is just what I don't want, Rushton. I don't want the police smelling in this. I want to avoid any publicity."

"That is always the blackmailer's strong card," muttered Rushton.

"I know. But I'll pay within reason. Yet, at all costs, I must avoid publicity. I—I have one strong reason beyond what I have told you."

Rushton glanced at him and saw that he was flushed deeper than his usual tan, and that his eyes held a shy expression. It was not difficult to guess the reason.

"There is—another lady in the case?"

"Yes. I wouldn't have her connected with a sordid police case for anything. Our engagement has not been announced. We were going to wait until I got a second divorce here in England. That would be easy now. Then we were going to be married quietly."

"I see. You wish to save her pain. Well, you may count on me, Errol. But I think I'd like to have a look at your guests and see what line they propose taking before making a suggestion."

"From this moment I leave myself entirely in your hands."

CHAPTER V   CROOKED GUESTS

RUSHTON and Tony had just finished dressing for dinner before the expected guests arrived.

They had been given delightful rooms, one on each side of a bathroom, which they shared, and, when he was ready, Tony wandered through to get Rushton before going downstairs.

They descended together to the big, comfortably furnished lounge hall, where a log fire was burning in the wide brick fireplace.

The moment they appeared, Mitsu glided in with a tray of cocktails, informing Rushton at the same time that his master had gone to the garage for a few moments but would soon join them.

Then, just before retiring, he turned his oblique eyes full on Rushton.

"The master's guests come soon now, sir."

Rushton held his gaze for a moment and nodded. He knew that Mitsu was in his master's confidence, but he did not know how fervently the little Jap hated the present Mrs. Richfield. Not even Errol knew that she had treated him with profound contempt in the past when he had resisted her attempts to suborn his loyalty from his master and from that time, when alone, had persisted in calling him. "Yellow dog."

Mitsu vanished, and scarcely was he gone when Errol came in. He picked up a cocktail, and the talk turned on casual subjects while they sipped.

But, very soon, there was the sound of a motor-siren outside, and Errol set down his glass.

"They are here, Rushton. I shall go and meet them."

Rushton and Tony nodded and drew back a little. The lounge hall in which they stood was really an inner hall connected with the outer hall by sliding glass-panelled doors.

But to go upstairs by the front staircase one had to enter the inner hall, the stairs being set over on the right-hand side to permit the place to be used as a lounge.

Where Rushton and Tony stood they could observe anyone in the outer hall without being seen and would not come into contact with persons coming through to mount the stairs.

They saw Errol pass through the outer hall to the vestibule and then disappear down the front steps. They saw Mitsu, now in a short black coat, enter the outer hall by another door there and hasten after his master. It was still just light enough outside for the inner hall to be comfortable for conversation without the lights being turned on.

There was a brief pause, and then they saw several persons enter the outer hall. Among them a woman stood out vividly. She was not tall, but was beautifully made and, even at the distance, one could be sure that her face was as beautiful as her figure.

She stood in very dark contrast to Errol, to whom she was talking and laughing vivaciously, and Rushton smiled grimly as he thought how Errol had said that she was an excellent actress off the stage as well as on.

A tall, thin man joined them, a man of long, saturnine features who was dressed in flashy American clothes. He seemed quite as much at ease as the woman and, certainly, Errol kept his end up as they came along the outer hall to the inner lounge.

Mitsu followed closely with a couple of suitcases, but when he was about half-way to the sliding glass doors which Errol had just opened, he was overtaken by another female figure who carried a leather jewel case and a rich-looking fur motor-wrap.

Mitsu stood aside to allow her to pass. She paused at the sliding glass doors and then murmured a word which gave her way past the others.

It was obvious that she was Mrs. Richfield's personal maid, and she seemed to know instinctively what she should do, for she made at once for the main stairs, leaving Mitsu to follow.

In that moment, during which she had paused by the sliding glass doors, however, Grant Rushton and Tony had had a clear view of her face. By the time she was on the stairs with the Jap following closely, Grant Rushton and Tony were looking at each other surreptitiously in incredulous amazement.

For, in that personal maid, they had recognised none other than the one-time opera singer and dancer, Gloria Ravissa, who had been known as the "Bird of Paradise" and had had all Paris at her feet, who, later, had become notorious as an adventuress and partner of that much more notorious master-criminal, "Flash" Brady.

"There's more, a lot more in this than just a blackmailing plot on the part of the Richfields," Rushton conveyed to Tony in a murmur that slid out of one corner of his mouth.

Then they were forced to turn and be introduced, for Errol and the Richfields were approaching.

But Rushton was right, even though the plot at work under the arrival of these people was not what he then might have thought, for it was one that not even the Richfields themselves guessed.

Tragedy, stark tragedy had been hovering, but was now getting ready to roost.

It would have been extremely embarrassing for an English divorced couple to meet with such complete *sangfroid* as was being exhibited by Mark Errol and Mrs. Richfield.

One in ignorance of the relationship in which they had once stood to each other would have found it impossible to conceive them as anything but host and welcome guest.

But Mark Errol had been long enough in America to become acclimatised, so to say, to the ways of the country and, even though he knew that the woman and man were his worst enemies—were out, indeed, to blackmail him for millions—he did not allow this feeling to appear in his smooth and courteous greeting. After all, he was a man of the world, and not an actor in melodramatics.

Nevertheless, Grant Rushton admired him for the manner in which he carried it off. It was not easy, and the more difficult, Rushton imagined, because the present husband, Richfield, was a very different stamp of person. Unless under conditions like the present he would never have been received in Errol's house.

In view of their journey and lateness of arrival, both the guests were excused from changing for dinner.

Richfield appeared before his wife, and lifted his saturnine brows when he was introduced to Rushton and Tony. At Rushton's special request, no secret was made of his identity.

But that the American crook didn't like the presence of the famous detective it was plain. His bravado immediately vanished, and he confined himself to cocktails and cigarettes until Mrs. Richfield appeared.

She, too, did not display any marked enthusiasm when Rushton was introduced, but she carried it off better than Richfield, and at dinner one would never have guessed that intrigue, plot and vile passions were seething beneath the suave manners of those at the table.

Errol had told Rushton that he proposed saying nothing about their reason for coming until they were gathered in the lounge. To this

Rushton agreed.

During the meal he made little attempt at conversation. His presence seemed to act as a restraint upon Richfield, but it had no such effect upon the woman.

After the first moment's uncertainty at meeting Rushton, she had quickly recovered her aplomb, and was now as vivacious as ever.

Certainly she had some reason for her self-confidence. She was unquestionably very beautiful, and Rushton could understand how she had always, or nearly always, had her way with any man with whom she came in contact.

At the same time he could see that she was completely under the control of Richfield, for from time to time she would send a quick, questioning glance in his direction, as if seeking his approval.

She and Errol discussed, mostly, happenings in New York, and Rushton made little attempt to talk to Richfield, for quite aside from entertaining an active dislike for the fellow, he was trying to figure out just where Gloria Ravissa came into the scheme of things.

Strictly speaking, Gloria Ravissa had occupied a higher social plane than Mrs. Richfield until the latter became the wife of Mark Errol. Gloria Ravissa had become outcast when joining "Flash" Brady, the notorious renegade from Scotland Yard.

Yet here was the one time celebrated "Bird of Paradise" acting as personal maid to Mrs. Richfield.

Rushton could not conceive that Gloria Ravissa had foresworn her former irregular ways in order to lead the humdrum existence of a maid.

Nor could he accept that she and Brady had parted company.

Then, what was she doing in her present role? Rushton had always gone on the theory that, where "Flash" Brady was, Gloria Ravissa could not be far away, and vice versa.

If that theory should still hold good, where was Brady at the present moment? Was this whole business that was being advanced by the Richfields not child of their brain at all, but the scheme of Brady? Were the Richfields only his tools? Did that explain why Gloria Ravissa was acting as maid?

If so, where was Brady?

Rushton realised, of course, that this was all pure surmise based on his own knowledge of the past. It might be susceptible to a very different explanation. But through all dinner he could not get out of his head the implications roused by the fact that the Richfields were undoubtedly crooks, and that Gloria Ravissa was in close association with the woman. For the first time, he was sorry that he had not approached the thing with more circumspection—a disguise and an assumed name. But, on the other hand, he was glad now that he had made no secret of his name when he wasn't disguised, for Gloria Ravissa would have no difficulty in recognising him and Tony.

When dinner was over and they were gathered in the lounge with coffee and liqueurs, Errol came to the point with almost brutal directness.

"Well, Carrie," he said abruptly, "perhaps you will be good enough to lay your cards on the table. If it will help you at all, I may tell you that I know all that has happened regarding my son. And I know you have not come to England for the pleasure of seeing me."

Rushton approved the opening. He, himself, was sitting back a little in the shadowy alcove at one side of the wide fireplace. Tony was close to him.

Errol was in a low leather chair at one side of the fireplace; Carrie Richfield in the one opposite. Richfield was somewhat between them.

The woman took up the challenge at once.

"I know that you have been in constant touch with the Kennedy man," she said coolly. "You certainly caught us napping at one time, Mark. But I think you will confess that the trump card lies with us now."

"Let us take all that for granted," responded Errol in a low tone, putting one hand up so that his eyes were shaded from the fire. "I am curious to know why you have done all this to me. Why did you suppress the fact of the birth of our son in the first place? Had I used you badly? Had I been niggardly in any way?"

The woman laughed lightly. The laugh told Grant Rushton that she was absolutely without heart, and was, as Errol had said, a gold-digger par excellence.

"Oh, dear no, Mark. Please do not get sentimental. I knew that we could not remain married for long. I will say that my first motive for keeping the matter secret was because I hated you. I did not want children. It spoiled my career, which was everything to me. Of course I should never have married you had it not been for your money."

"I learned that," he said quietly.

"Later on, I decided that the possession of a son might prove very useful. I had not intended that you should know so soon. It was that wretched girl, Jeanne, who precipitated matters."

"What did you intend, then?"

"To bring the boy up according to my own ideas. I do not like you English, as you know. I wanted him to be filled with my ideas before knowing that his father was English. Then I would make my own terms with you."

"That, at least, is frank enough."

Again she laughed, while Grant Rushton felt a wave of disgust engulf him.

The child, to her, was not flesh of her flesh and bone of her bone. It was nothing but a counter by which she might realise her greed for money.

"Of course I am frank. You and I are nothing to each other now. Darrell and I are completely congenial. But you can have the boy, Mark—at a price. I don't want the responsibility of the little beast any longer. You will be glad to get him because, heaven knows, he is enough like you."

Errol winced with pain, but kept his hand over his eyes.

"You say—at a price. Surely I offered you a large sum?"

"Not enough, Mark, not enough. I might have taken it once in my ignorance, but I did not know then how rich you were. We want more than that."

"How much?"

"Three-quarters of a million—pounds!"

Tony made an involuntary movement at the mention of such a colossal sum, but Rushton shot him a warning glance. Errol did not stir. Carrie Richfield was smiling over her cigarette. Darrell Richfield looked longer in the face and more saturnine than ever.

"What guarantee have I that, if I pay you such a sum as this, you will keep your part of the bargain?"

Here, Darrell Richfield spoke for the first time.

"You get the kid—isn't that enough?" he asked in a tone that was almost a whisper.

"But what guarantee that you leave him alone in future?"

"Say, Errol, what guarantee do you want? You've got witnesses here in a couple of detectives, haven't you? If you wanted to, you could send for the police and have us arrested for blackmail, couldn't you? Well, you're not going to do that, because if anything unhealthy happens to us, the kid gets snuffed out—quick. See? We didn't come all this way without taking proper precautions."

"How would you propose to hand over my— son?"

The woman took up the talk again.

"We've arranged that. I'll tell you this much— he's in New York. He can be handed over to your stool pigeon, Kennedy, at a word from us. But we don't give that word until we've seen the money. And listen, big boy, it's got to be in the form of real money. We don't want any cheques or drafts or anything that has any comeback."

"If I came to terms with you, I should not attach any strings," returned Errol curtly. "I want to talk this over with Mr. Grant Rushton. Will you excuse us for a few minutes?"

"Sure, Mark, go as far as you wish, as long as you don't try to double-cross us."

Errol made no response, but, rising, motioned to Rushton. Tony was left to keep an eye on the Richfields.

Rushton's host led him up the main staircase, where, in the gloom of the upper hall, Rushton thought he caught sight of someone just vanishing from view. But he could not be sure.

He thought of Mitsu, solicitous for his master's welfare, but at that moment he caught sight of the valet in the lower hall, his hands occupied with a tray on which were several bottles.

Then he thought of Gloria Ravissa. Had there been someone listening to what was being said in the lounge? And, if so, was it she? What other indoor servants did Errol employ? He could not answer that question just then, but he was to find it necessary to ascertain the number before many hours were passed.

They walked along the thickly-carpeted upper hall, past several closed doors, until Errol paused before one. The rooms occupied by Rushton and Tony were in the opposite direction.

Errol ushered Rushton into a small but very cosily furnished study, the walls of which were completely covered with laden bookshelves. He had been there before, and knew it for Errol's private retreat, to which he admitted few persons.

He sat down at a walnut desk and motioned Rushton into the low chair beside it. Then he took off the lid of a silver box of cigarettes and pushed them across.

"What do you think of it, Rushton?"

"It's about as good an example of stone-cold nerve as I have ever come across," was Rushton's blunt reply.

"I know. But—I am inclined to accept it. You heard their threat."

"To harm the boy?"

"Yes."

Rushton nodded. He could not bring himself to wave it aside. He knew that Richfield was perfectly capable of having made such arrangements, although his blood boiled to think that the crook dared to sit there so coolly and boast of it to Errol.

Yet what could be done? If he were to advise Errol to refuse entirely to treat with them, what would be the result? If the boy were not murdered out of hand, then he would be lost to Errol for ever.

If he were left to the mercies of that vile woman, she would take good care that he developed into just the sort of man Errol would not have him.

She herself possessed not a shread of wifely or maternal love. That was abundantly clear. Yet it went against Rushton sorely to see Errol hand over three-quarters of a million pounds to that pair of blackmailing crooks, rich though he might be.

"I don't know, honestly, what to advise," he said at last, very slowly. "My inclination says one thing; my sympathy with you and fear for the boy say another."

"Listen, Rushton. I am going to yield to their demands, preposterous though they are. I have in that safe in the corner British Government bearer bonds to the amount of five hundred thousand pounds. I have a further large sum at my bank in Henley. It happens that I brought some of these bonds down from London when I was first preparing to transfer the half million dollars to Kennedy, in case he could make terms. Since then I have had more sent down, because I was going to convert them into a new Government loan. The amount just answers their demands. You may think it weak, but since I heard that threat I am afraid—afraid."

Rushton shook his head.

"I don't think you weak, and I don't blame you, Errol. But it galls me to see them get away with three-quarters of a million like this.

"Can you suggest anything?"

"Nothing—except to run them in for blackmail and get in touch with Kennedy at once."

"But the child."

"I know. There is that risk. If they are not bluffing—"

"She is not bluffing. Nor is he. I am sure of that. She still hates me, Rushton—hates me like poison. She'd like nothing better than to strike such a blow if I took such steps."

"Then I am afraid I can suggest nothing, old man. But I should make very sure that they carry out their part of the arrangement before handing them over a penny."

"I shall. This is what I propose. If they agree to my suggestion, I shall put through calls to New York at once. I shall listen while they give instructions for the boy to be handed over to Bryant Kennedy. When Kennedy advises me that this has been done, then I shall pay over the bonds I have here in the safe, and to-morrow after a second confirmation from Kennedy that the boy is with him and safe, I shall hand over the balance of the quarter million. I can get the bonds from the bank in the morning. And I shall get you to draw me up a short paper, which we shall make them sign promising that this finishes the matter."

"I can do that," said Rushton grimly. "And I shall guarantee that they shall never be admitted to England again after they get out this time. I shall have them put on the black list."

"Thank you."

"This cuts me, Errol. I came down here at your request, and I agreed to use my efforts to stop this bunch mulcting you of any large sum of money. Yet here I am agreeing to your paying the best part of a million pounds. One thing, please make sure of—I will not be bound by any conditions that I am to take no steps to recover the money afterwards."

"I think they will feel too sure of themselves to worry about that, although I fear we shall have to guarantee them immunity until they are back in New York."

"I fancy so. But—after—we shall see."

They descended to the lounge, where Errol informed the Richfields that he agreed to their demands. He explained in detail how he proposed protecting himself, and they agreed without demur. But, that they were suspicious of the part Rushton was playing, was evident when the woman said:

"You've got to show us that there's going to be no backwash to this, Mark. Where does this detective friend of yours come in?"

"I have advised Mr. Errol to accept your offer," said Rushton brusquely. "It is blatant blackmail and, as you have admitted, you could be arrested for it in this country. And I may add that blackmail here is looked upon as one of the worst crimes. If it were not that the boy is in America and that we fully believe you capable of doing him a serious injury, my advice would be very different. Nor do I think it would avail to appeal to any sense of decency you may have or to maternal instincts."

"Lay off—lay off!" growled Richfield. "Don't talk to my wife like that. It's her kid, not yours."

"It's Errol's!" snapped Rushton.

"U-huh! For the price you named."

Rushton shrugged and, at Errol's request, laid down the conditions in detail. The Richfields agreed to everything, stating that the sooner they got out of England the better pleased they would be.

"We'll go ahead to-night," agreed the man, "but we must have some guarantee that we get the other quarter million to-morrow, and we've got to know that these bonds are the same as ready money. We ain't going to fool with anything that's got strings tied to it."

"There won't be any strings," explained Errol patiently. "I am ready to pass my word of honour that I shall keep my agreement to the letter. Carrie can tell you whether that can be depended upon or not."

The woman nodded.

"That's good enough," she drawled. "I'll say you're a 'right guy' that way, big boy."

"Well, let's get going."

Just at the back of the lounge hall, under the staircase, was a small room in which Errol had the telephone installed. Leaving Rushton with the woman, he took Richfield along to this room, and when the crook had supplied him with a certain New York telephone number, put through a trans-Atlantic call.

They did not return to the lounge while waiting, but remained in the telephone-room smoking, and within five minutes Rushton could hear the faint tinkle of the call bell.

In another five minutes or so the pair emerged. Rushton glanced at his host inquiringly.

"He has given instructions to someone in New York that the boy is to be taken to Bryant Kennedy's office," said Errol. "Will you get through to Kennedy, Rushton? Then we can settle the other part of the business."

Rushton turned to Tony.

"Put through a call to Kennedy, Tony."

It was, Rushton noticed, just ten o'clock, which meant that it was about five in the afternoon in New York; so unless Kennedy were out on some case, they ought to catch him at his offices in the old Flatiron Building.

As a matter of fact, it took Tony less time to get through than it had taken Richfield. Within a couple of minutes he was beckoning Rushton.

Rushton explained matters to Kennedy as briefly

"I wish you would stand by until the child is handed over."

"I'll do that," came back Kennedy, "and you can bet your sweet life they won't get him again. Give me your number and I'll 'phone through to you the moment the kid shows up."

Rushton gave him the number of Errol's house and the Henley exchange for a relay from London. Then he returned to the lounge.

At Errol's request he sat down at an old oak bureau in one corner and, switching on the desk-light, wrote out a draft agreement which he thought would cover the matter.

When he read it over, both Errol and the Richfields agreed to its terms. Errol took it and turned to the blackmailers.

"Well, let's get this thing signed," he said curtly.

"I'd like to see that half million first," drawled the woman.

"I am no trickster. You shall have the bonds the moment this is signed. They are in a safe in my private study. You can come and see them now if you wish."

She rose at once.

"That suits me, big boy. You can stay here and keep your detective friend company, Darrell."

Richfield frowned, but remained with Rushton and Tony. Rushton watched the two go up the stairs, thinking, as they disappeared, that Errol had certainly played a poor card when he first got tangled up with that gold-digger.

Then he lit a cigarette and ignored Richfield, although it was obvious that the crook would have been glad if he and Tony were not sitting over him.

Thus for perhaps five minutes. Then the three persons who sat in the lounge sat up with a jerk, as, muffled but plain enough to leave no doubt as to what it was, there came the single burst of a gunshot.

It was the sound of Errol's voice that brought Rushton to his feet. Richfield and Tony also sprang up.

"Rushton—Rushton, come quickly!"

Rushton raced across the intervening space of the lounge and took the stairs two at a time.

At the top was Errol, and even in the subdued lighting Rushton could see that he was deathly pale, and trembling from sudden shock of an acute form.

He gripped Rushton's arm until it hurt.

"My heavens, Rushton, come along! She— she— I don't know how it happened."

Rushton asked no questions. He saw Tony and Richfield now at the top of the stairs. He raced along the hall to the door of Errol's study, which was now wide open.

And the moment he paused on the threshold he saw what Errol had meant.

Lying on the floor, close to the desk, was Mrs. Richfield. She was on her back, with her knees drawn up a little owing to the pressure of her feet against the desk.

On the front of the light green frock she had been wearing, just over the heart, was a dark, sinister stain which could only have one origin.

It needed no more than that to tell Rushton that she was dead.

RUSHTON remained on the threshold until he had made a quick survey of the room.

When he removed his gaze from the woman, he saw, on the carpet close to her right hand, a small blued steel revolver, not an automatic pistol, just as if it had slipped from her grasp.

The next thing he saw was that the french windows were now wide open, allowing the soft night breeze to stir the curtains ever so gently. He remembered that, when he had been up there half an hour before, the windows had been closed.

He stepped over the threshold and walked swiftly to the windows. Outside was a narrow balcony that ran the full length of that side of the house.

He peered along its length, but it stretched quite empty. He turned back into the study just as there came a cry from the door, and Darrell Richfield sprang in from the hall.

Tony was trying to restrain him, but Richfield shook him off and knelt down beside the dead woman. In doing so he pushed the weapon aside, and got his arms about her, while, in complete unrestraint, he gave way to outcries that were unfitted to one of his sex.

But these broke off as abruptly as they had begun. Easing the body back to the floor, he grabbed the weapon and sprang to his feet, facing Errol.

"It was you who killed her!" he roared. "I'll show you how you get away with that, you—"

He threw up the weapon and tried to pull the trigger. But Rushton was too quick for him. Even before the movement of Richfield's arm he was springing forward, and catching the fellow's wrist he twisted it back swiftly and then jammed it up between his shoulder-blades.

The revolver fell to the floor, and Rushton forced Richfield into a chair.

"Listen," he said sternly, "we can understand that you are upset at what has happened, but you can't do that sort of thing in this country. However this may have occurred, it is not for you to upset the evidence as it lies. That is for the police. I will release you if you promise to remain quiet. If not, I shall have you forcibly restrained. Which is it? Hurry up, I am not going to waste time."

"Let me go!" was the smothered response. "I'll be quiet!"

Rushton released him and signalled to Tony to watch him. Then he noticed that Gloria Ravissa was standing at the door, staring at him noncommittally with her dark velvety eyes. She was in her maid's attire, on her left arm was some sort of filmy garment. Just behind her, watching his master, was Mitsu.

Rushton paid no attention to Gloria Ravissa then. He was engaged with the body of the woman, and in getting things replaced as they had been when he entered the room.

He picked up the revolver from where it had fallen and, while replacing it as nearly as possible as it had been, took note of the calibre, which he saw was not exactly common—.25.

But that was not all that he discovered in those few moments. He was handling the weapon as carefully as possible, knowing that the police would wish to treat it for finger-prints, and it was then that he realised something on which the whole case was to hinge.

But no one else knew anything about this as Rushton straightened up and turned to Errol.

He was about to speak when Mitsu stepped to the threshold.

"Telephone is ringing, master," he said, as unemotionally as if no dead body were within a hundred miles.

"I'll take the call," put in Rushton quickly. "It may be Kennedy. You, Errol, and you, Tony, see that nothing is disturbed until I come back."

Richfield made as if he would rise and protest against something, but changed his mind after a glance at the other two, and subsided.

Rushton pressed by Gloria Ravissa, who was standing just like any maid would stand until permitted to speak about this dreadful thing that had happened to her mistress. Neither took notice of the other.

Rushton strode along the hall and down the stairs. It was Kennedy on the transatlantic 'phone, as he hoped.

"I've got the kid, Rushton," he announced jubilantly.

"Stick to him, Bryant—stick to him," was Rushton's emphatic response. "I can't tell you what is going to happen yet, but Mrs. Richfield is dead."

"Dead! What on earth do you mean?"

"Just what I say. I don't know the facts yet —whether it is suicide or something else. I'll get in touch with you as soon as possible, but I can't remain now. But—keep that kid safe, at all costs."

"You can depend on me, old man."

And when Rushton hung up it was with a mind eased on at least one point, which was as well, for he was sorely troubled over another.

On regaining the upper floor, he found that Gloria Ravissa had disappeared. Errol had dropped into a chair. Tony was still standing guard over Richfield. Rushton gave his attention to Errol.

"What can you tell me about this, Errol?"

His voice was quite friendly but firm. He had already had time enough to realise several things.

One was that here before him was a dead woman who would be, he thought, the last person in the world to commit suicide and, more particularly, at a moment when she stood to benefit to the tune of three quarters of a million pounds. That sudden and acute remorse might have entered into the affair did not seem probable.

Yet what would the police say to that revolver which lay so close to her right hand?

Then there was the fact that several persons were on the upper floor at the time of the tragedy. Richfield might be capable of killing—Rushton did not doubt that for a moment—but he could be definitely ruled out, because he had been downstairs with him and Tony when the shooting took place. Moreover, Richfield had no apparent motive to engineer such a thing, unless—

And here Rushton paused to consider Gloria Ravissa. She, too, was capable of killing. And the possession of three quarters of a million pounds would be quite sufficient motive.

Was it possible that she and Richfield had intrigued together to allow Carrie Richfield to bring matters to a head, and then put her out of the way while they pocketed the million? It was worth thinking about.

And certainly Gloria Ravissa had been, not only on the same floor, but in close proximity when the deed was done. But, likewise, Mark Errol had been there. And Mitsu, who, Rushton was positive, hated Carrie Richfield as deeply as he was loyal to his master—where had Mitsu been? Then he remembered seeing Mitsu in the lounge with a tray when he raced up the stairs.

These things were passing in his detective's mind while he waited for Errol to speak.

"I hardly know what to say, Rushton," he heard Errol stammering. "We were in here—she was seated at my desk—we had just finished with the paper you drew up, and I was going along the hall to call you up as a witness when I heard the sound of a shot. I ran back and saw her on the floor; then I ran back to the head of the stairs and called you."

"She was quite normal when you left her at the desk?"

"Perfectly. I had just given her the bundle of bonds, and she had said something about the balance to-morrow."

"You had given her the bonds, you say?"

"Yes. While she was reading the agreement I took them from the safe."

Rushton looked on the desk, but could see no signs of any such certificates. But he did see a very large leather handbag which he knew to have belonged to the dead woman. She had had it with her in the lounge, and had taken it along when going upstairs with Errol.

"Do you know where she put them? Would they be in this bag?"

"Yes. After glancing at them and making some remark about hoping they weren't forgeries, she put them in that bag."

Rushton stepped to the desk and picked up the bag. At this point Richfield made another attempt to get up, but Rushton swung on him with a grim remark that sent him back. Then Rushton opened the bag and made a cursory inventory of the contents.

There was a good deal of junk inside such as women collect in their bags, but of anything in the nature of a bundle of British Government bearer bonds there wasn't a sign. There wasn't even one bond.

Rushton laid the bag back on the desk.

"Where are they now?" he asked abruptly, knowing that Errol had also seen that they were not in the bag. Then: "Better give me any details you can, old man."

"I can't think of much more, Rushton. That gun, I saw that in her bag when she opened it."

"Ah! It was her gun, was it?"

"I presume so."

"Of course it was!" burst out Richfield. "I gave it to her. Isn't it plain enough to you, you snooping gumshoe? Errol gets her up here and makes a play to hand over the bonds. He gets her to sign the agreement, and then when he's got her name in black and white he grabs the bonds and bumps her off."

"Be quiet! You'll have plenty of chance to say your piece to the police when they come."

"Police," muttered Richfield, "I don't want the police."

Rushton ignored him.

"Listen, Errol. We'll have to telephone to Henley and inform the police. I'm going to get through personally to Scotland Yard, but that doesn't mean that they will take a hand. It all depends on the country people. But I think the Yard ought to be in this, and I'm afraid, old man, that your desire for no publicity is shot to pieces."

"It doesn't matter—it doesn't matter. It was the boy and the other."

"The boy is safe now in Kennedy's hands, and will remain safe. As for the other"—Rushton knew he meant his fiancée—"she'll stick by you. Just how long a time elapsed from when you left the room until you heard the shot?"

"Only a matter of a few moments—maybe half a minute."

"Did you close the door after you?"

"Yes, I think so. I can't be sure."

"There was no one else about?"

"Why—no. I saw Carrie's—Mrs. Richfield's maid when I was hurrying back after hearing the shot."

"Where was she?"

"Just coming out of the room next door. That is the room I gave to Mrs. Richfield."

"When were the windows opened?"

"I don't know. They were open when we came in. I suppose Mitsu opened them."

"Mitsu never touched them, master."

This from the Jap, who was standing just outside the door.

"Well, they were closed when you and I were here," stated Rushton.

"Then I don't know."

Rushton regarded Mitsu for a moment. He had a feeling that the little Jap might be able to throw some light on the tragedy if he chose to talk, and yet how could he? He might feel inclined to kill the woman, but it was not within the limits of human possibility that he could have done so, and then got down to the other floor, picked up a tray of bottles and taken it into the lounge in such a short time.

What of Gloria Ravissa?

Rushton knew that he was treading on dangerous ground here. It was, of course, quite open to him to state publicly who she was and to give her record to the police.

That would at once put her under some suspicion and, at any rate, discredit her as a witness. But he was not ready to do that. As the thing stood, three things looked possible:

1. Carrie Richfield might have been seized with an acute attack of remorse and committed suicide.

If so, what had she done with the bonds? And, again, if that were so, how had she shot herself without scorching the front of her frock? In his first brief examination Rushton had taken note that there was no sign of powder marks.

2. Gloria Ravissa might have had some motive for killing the other woman.

If she had done the deed, how had she managed to carry it out and get into the next room so as to emerge just as Errol was coming back along the hall?

There were the open french windows and the balcony. She could come and go that way, but a certain space of time would be necessary, and Rushton did not believe that the time at her disposal would be sufficient.

3. Errol might have shot the woman who had done so much to ruin his life and that of their son.

But none of these suggestions accounted for the bonds. If Gloria Ravissa had done the deed, where had she put the bonds? If Errol was responsible, what had he done with them? No one had much time to waste over their disposal.

"Is the safe open?" asked Rushton abruptly.

"Yes."

"May I look inside?"

"Of course."

He went to the corner and, turning the handle, drew open the heavy door. Inside were several vertical compartments filled with account-books and bundles of papers. In the centre was a sort of inner safe, in the keyhole of which still hung a bunch of keys. Rushton opened it. There were several packets of bank-notes inside and other items which were germane to Errol's personal affairs. But there were no bonds such as he sought.

He turned back to Errol. What he was going to ask was, he knew, only a matter of form as far as he was concerned. But before the police came on the scene he wanted to see how Gloria Ravissa would answer his questions; whether she would betray any sign that they had met before, and whether any glance of communication would pass between her and Richfield.

"You agree that we notify the police, Errol?"

"Of course. It is for you to say what must be done, Rushton."

"I think that is our only course. I take it that you wish me to act for you?"

"Oh, indeed, yes!"

"Then I shall do so, and, as I said, I think we should make every effort to get Scotland Yard brought in."

"What about me?" demanded Richfield. "Where do I come in? What about my money?"

"Listen," said Rushton evenly. "The less you say the better it will be for you. I don't know whether you had foreknowledge of this deed or not. That may or may not come out. But your position is a most precarious one. Mr. Errol's boy is now in safe hands, so that club will be of no further use to you. Your blackmailing game has been sunk through this deed, and it remains with you whether you are taken up by the English police for blackmail with threats of bodily harm, or whether I smother that for the present. You must remain here until this matter is cleared up. It can be understood that you do so of your own free will, and the whole business will be confined to the investigation of your wife's death. Other things will have to come out, naturally—the former relationship between your late wife and Mr. Errol. But for the sake of everyone concerned, the other had better be kept in the background as much as possible. I have warned you. It is for you to make a fool of yourself if you wish to do so."

Rushton turned back to Errol, while Richfield subsided into a sulky but none the less dangerous silence. Rushton felt almost convinced now that the fellow had had no hand in plotting his wife's death. He also believed that he was definitely suspicion of Errol. In that state of mind there was no telling what he might do once he found himself regarded as a witness by the police.

But Rushton could not deal with that danger now. He knew that no time must be lost in getting through to the police. Yet he intended to question Gloria Ravissa while everything was hot.

"I'd like to question the maid," he said to Errol.

"Of course. Mitsu can get her."

46

"I am here, monsieur."

Gloria Ravissa had returned to the shadows in the hall, and Rushton knew that she must have overheard every word he spoke to Richfield. He invited her to come into the room.

She obeyed, her dark eyes, ever so slightly oblique from the Oriental-Javanese blood in her, measured his enigmatically. Rushton couldn't tell whether she intended to reveal their former knowledge of each other, or whether she intended to take his line.

"How long have you been personal maid to the late Mrs. Richfield?" was his first question.

"About six months, monsieur."

"What can you tell us about this unfortunate tragedy?"

"Very little, monsieur. I was in madame's room, preparing her things for the night. I heard what sounded like a shot, and opened the door. I saw Monsieur Errol in the hall. Then I looked in the room and saw madame. I was very frightened, and returned to the other room."

"That is all?"

"Yes, monsieur."

"When you saw Mr. Errol in the hall, which way was he walking?"

She hesitated for the veriest fraction of time before replying:

"He was hurrying towards the stairs, monsieur."

Errol sat up.

"What nonsense, girl! When I saw you I was running back to discover the cause of the shot."

"I am sorry, then, monsieur. I saw monsieur first when he was leaving this room and hastening towards the stairs."

Rushton's face stiffened to a threatening grimness. His eyes bored into the dark orbs of the woman, which now seemed to be mocking him.

This was a very serious statement she had just made. It was in direct conflict with what Errol said, and it insinuated that she had seen him running from the room immediately after the shot was fired — hinting, in fact, that, privily, she thought he had done the shooting.

Rushton believed Errol. He knew Gloria Ravissa was deliberately casting suspicion upon him. And in doing so she had revealed a cold nerve; for, in order to discredit her as a witness before the police, all he had to do was to reveal her identity and record.

Yet she had risked that. Why? She must have sensed intuitively that he did not intend to reveal his knowledge of her, and she had cornered him now by this daring statement.

She knew that he did not want to give her away. She could not know why. Nor did anyone else in that room know what Grant Rushton had in his mind.

Nor could Gloria Ravissa dream that Rushton had made a discovery which—did he choose to reveal it now—would eliminate Errol at once as a guilty possibility, would tend to incriminate her if he could prove that she had had time to rush from this room to the balcony, through the next room and into the hall between the time of the shooting and when Errol saw her enter the hall.

That was a thing, though, that must be approached with utmost care. It was a thing which Rushton had no intention should be laid before the police yet, not even if his client, Mark Errol, should be arrested on suspicion.

For Grant Rushton did not believe that the shot had been fired inside the house. Why?

Because he was ready to bank his reputation that the weapon on the floor was not the one that had been used to kill Carrie Richfield.

Again, why?

Because, when he took the weapon away from Richfield, barely a minute after the sound of the shot, he would have found, had it been the weapon used, that the barrel was still hot. It was a revolver that used only cordite-loaded cartridges. One discharge would be quite sufficient to heat the barrel to a considerable degree from breech to muzzle.

But the blued steel had been perfectly cold!

CHAPTER VII   THE TRAIL IN THE NIGHT

SHORTLY after midnight Mark Errol was asked to go with the police to Henley police-station.

The events leading up to this request followed almost exactly the outlines Grant Rushton had forecast.

Following his telephone message to the police, Rushton had had a line-up of those servants immediately connected with the house. In addition to Mitsu there were:

Mrs. Dean, a woman of fifty-odd, who acted as housekeeper and cook. Millie Dean, her daughter, who assisted her mother and did the duties of housemaid and parlourmaid, which were light enough in that establishment, where Mitsu attended to practically everything connected with his master. Liddle and Stevens—chauffeur-mechanics, who were fully occupied with looking after Errol's five cars and his private aeroplane. Hall, a groom who cared for the two riding-horses which Errol kept.

In addition to the above there were three gardeners and two keepers, who lived in cottages in the village. There was no extensive shooting attached to the estate, but the keepers found most of their work with the fishing, the few birds, mostly partridges and some wildfowl, which Errol bred along the string of three lakes.

The two chauffeur-mechanics and the groom were all unmarried, and slept in rooms above the large garage at the rear of the house. This garage, in fact, was a converted coach-house.

At Rushton's request they were summoned to the kitchen. The evidence they could give was not very helpful.

Mrs. Dean, a buxom, pleasant-looking woman, had been in her private sitting-room most of the evening. This room adjoined the kitchen, and, by its position, was somewhat distant from the front part of the house.

She had heard nothing. Her daughter Millie had been with her, and her evidence was as negative as that of her mother but for one thing. Somewhere about twenty minutes past ten the dead woman's maid had come down to the kitchen to get some boiling water. This must have been before the shooting, Rushton figured, for he timed the shot as having been fired at just about twenty-two minutes past ten.

Millie Dean had given the other maid what she asked for and had then returned to her mother; but she had heard no shot.

Liddle had been over at the landing-ground, at work in the hangar. He had heard nothing.

Stevens, the chauffeur, who had brought the Richfields from Henley Station, stated that he had gone to bed about half-past nine and woke somewhere after ten. He opined that it might have been the sound of a shot that woke him, but he could not say for sure.

Hall, the groom, had gone to bed about nine, and had slept right on until he was summoned by Liddle to come to the kitchen.

So much for the evidence of the servants.

Rushton had completed this examination when the police arrived from Henley. There was an inspector—Inspector Blain—and a sergeant. Already at the house was the local village constable, who had been fetched by Hall, the groom.

From this point Rushton retired into the background. He had a hunch what line of thought would be followed by the police, and he did not wish to say or do anything that would make matters worse for Errol. And, certainly, he had to confess that, on evidence, matters looked black enough against his host.

Quite aside from other things, there was the question of the bonds. No one but Errol could say anything about them. There was only his word as evidence that there had been any bonds at all. With the other evidence it was an easy step to the point where one could question their existence, and then to the next point where one might suggest that there had been no bonds in the safe, but that Errol had used that statement as a lure to get the woman alone in his study so as to stage the crime. Motive he had in plenty.

And this was exactly the channel of deduction which Inspector Blain took.

Ordinarily, Rushton's presence would have been welcomed by most country inspectors, but for some reason or other, Blain was by no means cordial.

Hence, Rushton was not much surprised when, after examining the servants, he turned to Rushton and said:

"It seems that you have anticipated me, Mr. Rushton. How does this come?"

"I questioned the servants as Mr. Errol's authorised agent," said Rushton curtly.

"Oh, so he has retained you already, has he? Well, do you care to make a statement, Mr. Errol? I should, of course, warn you that anything you say may be taken down in writing and used as evidence should there be any charge against you."

"Does this mean that I am under arrest?" asked Errol quietly.

"No—not yet. But I am going to ask you to accompany us to Henley police-station."

"Very well. I shall make a statement there."

He glanced at Rushton, who nodded approval.

Rushton made no mention of Scotland Yard. But, while the local men were busy examining the study, he descended to the telephone-room under the stairs and put through a call to Major Holden, Chief Constable of the Bucks County Police, who lived at Slough.

His conversation with that gentleman was brief, but when he closed off it was with the assurance that Major Holden would come to Henley early in the morning, and then come out to Fingest Grange.

The body of the dead woman was laid on the couch in the study until details about the inquest should be decided. The room was closed and sealed, and the two adjoining rooms were treated in similar fashion.

The sergeant and local constable were left at the house, and while no official restraint was in evidence, all those in the house were informed that they must remain as material witnesses.

Rushton made no comment of any kind. When the police car was ready to take Errol in to Henley, he turned to Blain.

"I am going in also, inspector. I wish to be present when Mr. Errol makes his statement."

"There won't be room in the car."

"That doesn't matter. I shall drive one of Mr. Errol's. I have sent Tony to bring it."

The inspector shrugged and turned away.

Tony appeared at that moment driving Errol's sports car, but it was Rushton who took the wheel.

He had already had a private talk with the lad, telling him what he wished him to do in his absence, so by the time the police car went down the drive Rushton was close after it.

The thing had boiled down to a simple choice of which story to believe—that of the maid, Gloria Ravissa, or of Errol.

Rushton could have discredited Gloria Ravissa by revealing her identity. On the other hand, there was no guarantee that this would be of any particular service to Errol.

Rushton believed that he could, at the right moment, submit evidence that would ensure Errol's release. But this was not the time to present it. The inspector would listen to nothing so technical then, and it would be as well to save it for the inquest.

Moreover, Rushton was defining his theory more and more clearly, and he did not want to put Gloria Ravissa too much on guard. It was taking a risk, he knew, and he was to discover on his return that he had not miscalculated there.

Tony knew a good deal of what was in Rushton's mind. Despite the presence of the sergeant from Henley and the local constable, it was his job to keep a watch on those who remained in the house. The police regarded Gloria Ravissa and Darrell Richfield merely as material witnesses. Tony and Rushton looked upon one at least as actively guilty in the killing, although Rushton did not consider it was her hand that had fired the shot. His startling theory was not to become public until the inquest.

But with Gloria Ravissa under sharp suspicion it was natural that Tony should confine his surveillance to her.

As soon as his examination was over, Richfield was permitted to retire to his room. After all, he was regarded by the police as the husband of the dead woman, and therefore entitled to certain sympathetic consideration. They did not know yet that he and the woman had come to England to extract heavy blackmail. Errol in his statement had simply said that the dead woman was his former wife, and that their business had been of a private nature to do with the past. Rushton had conveyed to him to say no more than that for the present.

And there was plenty of evidence that Richfield could have had no hand in the shooting. Indeed, Darrell Richfield was one of the most puzzled persons in that house of tragedy.

He still believed that Errol had shot and killed his former wife, and his suspicions even went so far as to include Rushton in the thing as a frame-up. His experience with detectives had been of an unfortunate nature. He regarded all of that profession from the same angle, and, certainly, he had been up against a good many in the States who would have framed a killing if the fee were big enough.

Therefore he believed that the whole thing was crooked between Rushton and Errol, but he had sense enough to keep his mouth shut on that score.

He was in deep water, and sorely desired a private conversation with Gloria Ravissa. He was in a strange country, where all police procedure was utterly strange to him.

He had read how serious blackmail was looked upon in England as a crime, and he felt as if he didn't know which end of the string to catch hold of.

The scheme to visit England and blackmail Errol was none of his devising. Back in New York he and his wife had met "Flash" Brady, and when Brady heard what a potential gold mine the Richfields had in Mark Errol, his fertile brain was soon at work.

Brady himself had been in England for some months making ready. The kidnapping of Errol's son by Bryant Kennedy had given a bad setback to his plans. But the re-kidnapping of the child had put them just where they were before, and he had lost no time in getting the Richfields to England with Gloria Ravissa acting as maid.

Grant Rushton did not know that Brady had met them in London and that everything since then had been at his direction. But Rushton did guess that Brady was mixed up in the thing, and further suspected what Darrell Richfield never dreamed— that Brady and Gloria Ravissa were double-crossing him.

But Brady had not been in evidence, and until he could make sure on that point Rushton was going cautiously.

Thus, all at sea as he was, Richfield hoped for a word with Gloria Ravissa. He was intensely worried about the missing bonds. He didn't know whether to sit tight or whether to make a break to escape.

But if he hoped to get hold of that shrewd little criminal adventuress this night, he was mistaken. She was otherwise engaged, as Tony was to discover, and Richfield dared not leave his room.

The upper hall ran, as has been said, in each direction from the top of the main staircase, rooms opening from each side.

The suite occupied by Rushton and Tony was along to the right, and if one continued in that direction one found that the passage turned and reached the rear or servants' staircase. Here, too, was another flight that led to the top floor, where the servants' bedrooms were located, although the only person who slept up there was Mitsu. Mrs. Dean and her daughter shared a large double bedroom off the housekeeper's sitting-room, while the men slept over the garage.

To the left of the main staircase were the rooms occupied by Errol himself, the study which has already been described, the bedroom next to it which was given to Mrs. Richfield, then came a bathroom and a smaller room which was occupied by Gloria Ravissa. On the other side of the hall were some unoccupied rooms and the one which had been given to Richfield.

This arrangement was all clear in Tony's mind as he re-entered the house and idled about the lounge until things should settle down. When he was satisfied that Richfield and Gloria Ravissa were in their rooms for keeps, he said good-night to the sergeant, who had taken up his position in the inner lounge, leaving the local constable in the outer hall, and went up to his room.

His first idea was to leave his door open a little and draw up a chair, from which he could keep a surveillance of the whole length of the upper hall.

But he soon discarded that, for he realised that if Gloria Ravissa should be up to mischief, she would be too canny to leave herself open to such easy discovery.

He did not know quite what to expect, if anything. It was quite on the cards that, having cast definite suspicion upon Errol by her flat contradiction of his story, she would sit tight.

There was, of course, the possibility that she might want to hold secret communication with Richfield, and Tony did not see how she could do that without either coming along the hall to his room, or having him go by the same way to hers.

But Rushton had been strongly of the opinion that, if Gloria Ravissa communicated with anyone, it would be with her partner "Flash" Brady. And Rushton was very certain now that Brady was somewhere close to the Grange.

"It was Brady who fired that shot, young 'un," he had stated with conviction. "We've got to find him, and as soon as I get back from Henley we'll begin. But we've got to have daylight."

Tony realised, on the other hand, that if Gloria Ravissa should try to communicate with him during the night, she might lead him to Brady if he could out-guess her.

He knew she would not make such a fool play as to descend into the hall and ask the police permission to go out for an airing or some other such excuse. Their orders were definite that no one who might be a material witness was to leave the premises. This, of course, did not apply to Tony.

At the same time Tony did not want the two men below to know what he was up to, so when he gave up his spying by the door, he took off the clothes he had been wearing and got into a flannel suit, putting on a pair of rubber-soled tennis shoes.

Then he turned out his light and opened his window. He knew it was a simple matter to drop to the ground, for beneath the balcony window was the soft soil of a flower-bed, the drop being not more than twelve feet. He did not worry about getting back. If he had to come by way of the door, he could make up some tale for the constable in the outer hall.

He landed as easily as he had anticipated, and dodging into the deep shadow, made his way right along the front of the house, so that he could keep a watch on the window of Gloria Ravissa's room.

He located the room firstly, by counting the windows along from the right hand side of the porch, and secondly, by the fact that it was the only room in the front that showed a light against the drawn blind.

But that light disappeared almost at once. Tony drew back into the still deeper shadows, and waited. It might be that the occupant of the room had finished her preparations for the night and was getting into bed.

On the other hand, it might mean that she was preparing for some strenuous activity. There was no telling what Gloria Ravissa might do.

The night was very still. Overhead the stars were bright, with a late, waning moon just above the horizon, soon the shadows which now gripped everything about the place would retreat before the growing light of the moon.

Then the silence was punctured by a tiny sound. It came from close to where Tony crouched, but he couldn't be sure just what it was until, up on the narrow balcony, he made out the dark blur of a figure against the window of the room he had been watching.

Gloria Ravissa was outside, and she had emerged as silently as he had managed the same job.

The blur grew smaller, but Tony could see it still as a blot against the window, and then it made a distinct movement. It was plain that the person, whoever it might be, was leaving the house in the same manner he had chosen.

The drop to the ground was the finished work of someone light and athletically springy. He had no doubt now that it was Gloria Ravissa, and he held his breath while she recovered and crossed into the shadow not a dozen feet from where he crouched.

Tony was too old a hand at the shadowing game to make a precipitate move. He waited, knowing that she would almost certainly do what he would do under the same circumstances—wait to see if her movements had been observed.

The minutes passed, but still he did not move. His ears were cocked to the slightest sound, and when the tell-tale noise of movement came, he knew that he had been wise.

She moved with a stealth that he could not but admire. Yet now and then the slight cracking of a twig, and, a little later, the soft crunching of a foot upon gravel, gave him as much clue as if she were shouting to him how she were going.

Tony had no doubt now that Brady was her objective. He could not tell whether she was just going for a brief conference and would then return to the house, or whether it was a clean getaway. If it were the latter, he had no instructions from Rushton advising him how he should act.

He thought of the half-million in bearer bonds. The police were inclined now to be sceptical that they had ever been in the safe and had been handed over to the dead woman. Rushton had not tried to persuade them to think differently. But both he and Tony believed Errol implicitly, and Tony could not help but wonder now if Gloria Ravissa was getting away with the goods. No particular search had been made for the bonds outside of Errol's study. That was a duty that was to be performed too late.

It was not until he was in fear of losing his quarry that Tony started from his place of hiding.

By skirting the path that ran along the front of the house, he was able to proceed with scarcely a sound, and, a few yards on, he came to the branching path which he knew must be the one where he had heard the crunch of Gloria Ravissa's shoe.

He then flattened himself into the shadows as he saw, some distance ahead, the momentary flash of a torch.

"A bit reckless that," he thought to himself. "But it's as good as a guide to me."

He moved on again, keeping to the velvety grass, and when he saw the brief flash of the torch a second time, knew not only that he was going right, but that he was gaining on his quarry.

From his previous stay at the Grange, he knew that this path ran down through the grounds to a little rustic bridge that crossed the stream. From there one could reach a summer-house that looked out upon one of the lakes. Beyond that the path continued to the high road that ran up through the valley towards Oxford. The main area of the estate lay to the other side of the house, over where the landing ground had been laid out.

Now Tony could see a clear light that seemed to hang right up in the sky. He glanced at it in a puzzled way, at a loss to account for it until, suddenly, he remembered that, high on a hill that overlooked the valley road was an old windmill that, he had been told, had been converted by an artist into a studio and living abode. It must be that the artist kept late hours, he was thinking, for, certainly, that light came from high up in the windmill.

But he had little time to give to that, for he knew now that Gloria Ravissa must be heading towards the rustic bridge. What was her purpose? Was Brady somewhere out there waiting for her?

That she was uncertain of her way was evident from the frequency with which she made use of the torch. But that she also had a good general idea of the lay of the place was equally evident from the certainty with which she had chosen her direction.

Tony saw the torch go on and off once more when, from his own calculations, he figured that she must be very close to the bridge.

He moved ahead even more quickly now, for the grass was soft and he made not a sound in his rubber-soled shoes.

By the time he reached the bridge she was nowhere to be seen, and he had no definite proof that she had crossed it. But he decided to take a chance and, feeling ahead cautiously for foothold, stepped off the grass on to the fine gravel that paved the approach to the planks.

He knew that, were she to stop on the other side and look back at that moment, she must see the blur of his figure against the skyline. But that was a risk he had to take.

He made the crossing as quickly as possible, and was just in the act of stepping off the other end of the bridge when, from out of the shadows on his left, something, seemingly gigantic, rushed out upon him.

Tony stiffened himself instinctively to meet the shock, but he was caught while in actual movement, and the bulk struck him with such force and weight that he was bowled clean over.

He went down fighting like a wild cat, and trying to get at his gun. But his mysterious assailant had anticipated every move that was possible, and crushed down upon him with such force that he was nearly smothered.

Then came a succession of savage blows that caught the lad about the face and head, battering him, confusing him, half stunning him.

He knew that his assailant was not Gloria Ravissa. No woman could have overwhelmed him with such weight and force as this.

Which meant that it was someone who had been lying in wait for her, had spotted him as he crossed the bridge, and, letting her pass on, had jumped him.

Who could it be but Brady?

That was the question that buzzed through his buzziness as he struggled with fast-ebbing senses to roll out from under those sledge-hammer blows.

But Brady or some other, his assailant, had no intention that he should escape. The attack continued with increasing rather than lessening violence and a particular brutal smash to the jaw was the last one needed to lay him quiet in a complete knockout.

A light stabbed the darkness, falling on Tony's upturned face.

From behind the glare came a sharp imprecation; then the light vanished.

"Where are you?"

The whisper cut the stillness and from somewhere in the gloom came the answer.

"Just here."

"Come along here."

The light flashed once more, then the blur behind it became merged with the shadows. The man who had been crouching above Tony had moved back.

Stealthily the blur that was Gloria Ravissa joined him. They blended as one while Brady, for Tony had guessed right, put his lips close to her ear.

His words were scarcely more than a breath.

"I waited until you went by to see if you were followed. Do you know who this is?

"Tony?"

"Yes. How did you know?"

"He is the only one who could have followed me, but I did not know he was behind."

58

"He'll never follow you again," he returned grimly. "Is everything all right?"

"Yes. They have taken Errol along to Henley. They'll arrest him all right. I settled him with my story."

"Good girl. What about Rushton?"

"He went with him. He is acting officially for Errol."

"Much good it will do him. We'd better get away at once. What about Richfield?"

"He's all at sea—in his room. He doesn't know what to make of it. He thinks Errol shot her."

"Things couldn't break better."

"Grant Rushton recognised me at once, but I called his bluff."

"That was the play. We'll be so far away by daylight, that he won't matter."

"He is suspicious just the same."

"Let him suspect all he wants to. Did he place the gun all right?"

"Everything went without a hitch. Richfield grabbed the gun, but Rushton took it away from him." Brady was silent for a few moments.

"Do you think he noticed anything?" he asked at last.

"I don't think so. He put it back on the floor at once. He didn't say anything."

"That was the only weak link in the whole chain so long as you did your stuff in good time."

"I did. I was through the window as soon as the shot was fired. I had the bonds, dropped the gun on the floor, and was out through the window again while Errol was still along the hall. My statement made him look a deliberate liar."

"That'll hold him until they uncover something, and they won't do that unless Grant Rushton smells a rat."

"Did you get the packet all right after I threw it from the balcony?"

"Sure. I watched some of the fun through the window. But I didn't stay long. No one thought to look in the grounds. That was one time I fooled Rushton to a standstill."

But Brady was wrong. Rushton had concluded long since that the fatal shot had been fired through the window, and his evidence at the inquest was to show this to be so.

"What are you going to do with Tony?" she whispered.

"I'd stick a knife in his gullet if I had one with me. I don't want to use a gun now. I can finish him off with my hands."

"Why not just pitch him into the stream? If he is knocked out that will finish him off."

"Not a bad idea. I'll do it."

"Have we got to go back to the windmill?"

"No. I fixed everything there. I'd have gone back if that brat hadn't turned up, but I guess we'd better get going. There's no telling how soon Rushton will be back from Henley. I hope Liddle is ready."

"He ought to be. He's been in the hangar all the evening, and went back there after he was called into the house to be questioned."

"Good."

She caught his arm as he moved.

"I don't trust that Japanese servant of Errol's. He may be snooping around."

"I'll fix him if he is. Sit tight for a minute until I get rid of this carrion."

He caught hold of the unconscious Tony and dragged him down under the bridge. He knew what the stream was like there, for Brady had spent many weeks in the converted windmill posing as an artist and preparing carefully for this great coup which at last he had pulled off.

Therefore he knew that the water flowed fairly swiftly, and was deep just below the bridge—a good place into which to push his victim.

Tony made no resistance. He knew nothing of what was going on. He was as limp as a sack of bran while Brady heaved him over the bank and eased him into the water so as not to make a splash.

Then he crawled back by the bank, and, by a side path he knew well, started to skirt the home park in order to reach the hangar at the landing-ground.

With the exception of a faint glow that came out of the front end of the hangar the landing-ground was in darkness. As they approached the entrance they could see Liddle, one of the chauffeur-mechanics working over a vice at a table.

To anyone watching him, it would simply appear that here was a fellow who was more than ordinarily conscientious about his work, who cared not for hours, and who was not even to be put off by the fact that there had been a murder close at hand.

But Liddle was Brady's creature, had been cleverly planted in the job by Brady after the former senior mechanic had been "forced" to leave through illness.

Inside the hangar Errol's nifty three-seater Bat stood ready to run out on to the ground. Beyond the landing ground the moon was now some distance above the horizon. Brady could not have chosen a better night had he had the choice. But the moon wouldn't have mattered, for a single turn of a switch would flood the ground with light which made a take-off or landing almost as simple as by day.

Liddle glanced up as they entered, and, seeing who it was, laid down his tools. He came across to them swiftly.

"Everything okay?" he whispered.

Brady nodded.

"Are you ready?"

"Been ready for hours."

"Then let's get going. Not a minute to waste."

"Climb in," was the laconic reply.

There was a sudden terrific uproar of sound as Liddle swung his propeller. It seemed fairly to lift the hangar from the ground. It was, the three knew, a definite advertisement that someone was taking a 'plane away from the ground, but it didn't matter.

Long before anyone could reach the spot Liddle was in his place, had shot his gun, was taxiing out across the ground, and then had lifted the Bat into the air.

He banked just once before shooting over the top of the trees, then he was away, circling as he climbed swiftly into the heavens. Less and less did the roar of the engine shatter the night above the house of murder. Slowly but steadily the drone died away while a startled sergeant of police and a bewildered village constable stood outside the Grange trying to figure out what was taking place.

They were still standing there when a second uproar shattered the night, and this time they saw a fierce glow of light in the direction of the landing-ground, followed by the silvery shape of a Puss Moth as it zoomed up and up, and then shot away to the south.

CHAPTER VIII   THE MAN WHO SUSPECTED

GLORIA RAVISSA was correct in feeling great distrust of Errol's Japanese valet Mitsu.

Right up to the moment of his master being taken away by Inspector Blain no one could have read anything of his emotions in the flat Oriental countenance.

If he felt grief at this thing that had befallen his master, he gave no sign. If he were indifferent, his face would have been the same expressionless mask.

Nevertheless, inwardly he was seething with rage and grief at this ghastly disgrace that had come upon his master. He knew that Mark Errol was incapable of cold-blooded murder, let alone killing a woman.

And, like Rushton, he had a strong suspicion of the smooth-speaking maid whose words had been accepted by the police before his master's statement.

He did not know what force was at work outside the house, but his Oriental capacity for analysing a thing along very different lines from the way in which a European brain would have worked had brought him to the same conclusion as Rushton.

He knew that whatever could be done for his master Rushton would do. His best service would be in trying to find some clue about the place, something that would link up the people inside the house with the force outside.

He felt no sorrow over the death of Carrie Richfield. He hated her living, and he hated her dead. Had it come to a point of what he considered necessary, he would cheerfully have finished her off with his own hands.

And when he realised that his master was actually suspected by the police, it was in his heart and mind to step forward and confess that he had done the shooting.

But he had refrained in time. Instinct told him that to make such a statement would be a disservice to Errol. He knew that investigation must show that he could not have been on the spot when the shot was fired. In fact, he had no more than left the dining-room with the tray of bottles. And something about Rushton's quiet manner, his cool acceptance of the police decision, warned him that he had better do nothing to cause complications.

So he devoted himself to keeping an eye about the place, and in pursuance of his suspicion that the murder was linked up with an outside force, he left the house as soon as he thought it safe to do so.

He had no need to go by the front door. Nor did he attempt to make his exit by the back door, which incidentally had been locked and the key taken by the police-sergeant.

Mitsu knew a way worth a dozen of such public means. When he had chosen his moment, he slipped down into the kitchen, and in the darkness unlocked the door leading to the wine cellar, of which he always kept the key.

From this place there was a small window through which he could crawl out into a sort of little bay at the back of the house, and from here it was a simple matter for him to reach the front.

What he might have done then is problematical, for he had no definite plan in view, and it is likely that he would have witnessed the surreptitious escape of Gloria Ravissa had it not been for Tony's unexpected departure by way of his bedroom window and the balcony.

As a matter of fact, when the lad dropped into the flower-bed, he landed not ten feet away from where Mitsu was crouching.

Mitsu knew the figure for that of Tony; but he did not indicate his presence there, for he did not know what Tony was up to, and he had no wish to spoil whatever it was. He knew that Tony, like himself, was working on behalf of Mark Errol.

Thus it came about that the trailer was trailed. Right along the front of the house Mitsu followed Tony, and when the lad went to earth almost directly beneath the window of Gloria Ravissa's room, the Jap also took cover.

Mitsu was a most efficient valet, but he would have been even more efficient as a detective. His trailing of Tony was a masterepice of quiet progression.

Like Tony, he had seen Gloria Ravissa drop from the balcony to the flower-bed. He knew the lad was following her, and, counting Tony as a friend, he did not wish to spoil his game.

But he moved ahead bit by bit, following the progress of the other two with an exactitude that was uncanny.

He was only a few yards away when Tony was attacked by Brady. Mitsu heard the sound of a struggle, but here his understanding failed to serve him.

He was confused. He could not believe that Gloria Ravissa had turned upon the lad, nor could he believe that Tony had precipitated matters by rushing upon her.

He guessed correctly that a third human element had entered into the affair, and realised suddenly that here must be the outside force which he suspected.

He crept forward again, eager to make sure of what was going on. He reached the bridge just when the struggle was finished.

He did not know what had happened. He could hear faint sounds just across the stream, but that was all.

He flattened himself to the ground and crawled down the bank to the edge of the water. He knew the value of water surface as a sounding-board, and here, despite the guarded manner in which Brady and Gloria Ravissa were talking, he managed to hear enough to tell him what was being planned, and to enlighten him considerably as to what had taken place at the time of the crime.

He knew now, too, that Tony had had the worst of the fight. He heard Brady say that he would knife the lad if he possessed the necessary weapon.

At this Mitsu half rose, his hand reaching beneath his jacket for his own long-bladed knife. But he paused as he heard what followed.

He was flat against the ground again when Brady rolled Tony into the stream. Nor did he move until the pair had crossed the rustic bridge and gone off in the direction of the landing-ground.

But as soon as he knew they were well away, he slid into the stream, and, knee-deep, began to wade, bending forward and searching with his hands as he did so.

They encountered what he sought where it was held for a moment against a protruding tussock of weedy turf. He got his arm about the lad's unconscious form and dragged him to the bank and up on to the grass at the top.

Then Mitsu set to work to apply the Japanese system of reviving the unconscious, working from the waist upwards instead of directly on to the barrel of the torso.

Smoothly his pliant fingers kneaded in under the diaphragm, forcing that muscular wall up and down so as to function against the lower lobes of the lungs.

He did not know whether Tony was unconscious only through a heavy blow, or whether he had in addition swallowed a quantity of water. But the system would serve both effects, for the kneading was directly upon that major nerve centre known as the solar plexus.

He had his reward far sooner than he expected. As a matter of fact, while Brady's last savage blow had been a clean knockout, it was just a little less in force than Brady had calculated, and Tony's powers of recuperation were greater than normal. Moreover, the treatment that Mitsu was applying was the very thing needed.

Tony was still dizzy and confused when he sat up. Some recollection of his struggle still remained uppermost in his mind, for, finding Mitsu, as he thought, manhandling him, he began to hit out, clumsily but savagely.

Mitsu got a mild ju-jitsu hold on him and began to speak. Presently the facts began to penetrate the lad's clearing brain.

"It's you, Mitsu," he jumbled. "Sorry. What's happened? Where am I? Oh, I remember! Where's Brady?"

"Two persons have gone to landing-ground, master. They plan to take Errol master's flying-machine. Mitsu thinks that Liddle is a traitor, for they speak of him waiting."

Tony's mind was clear enough now. He cocked his ears at the Jap's words, and began to get to his feet.

"So that's it, is it? Well, I'll show them that two can play that trick. Which is the quickest way to the landing-ground, Mitsu? And what are you doing here, anyway? It seems to me I'm owing you some thanks."

"Mitsu was only looking about like master. Saw master following woman from house, and went after master. Shortest way to landing-ground is through path close at hand. If master will come—"

"You can show me the way, Mitsu, but you must go back to the house. Listen: If the police know you are out in the grounds, they will think you are doing something secret for Errol master. And that will injure him. These local police in my country are always suspicious of foreigners, Mitsu. So if you wish to help Errol master, you must go back."

"Very well, master, I obey," was the submissive reply. "But, first, I show master the way."

"Come along—no time to lose."

They re-crossed the rustic bridge, and Mitsu guided Tony into a side path.

"If master follows this and, when he comes to a branch, takes

65

turning to left, he will come out beside shed where air machine is kept," he whispered.

"All right. I'll use my torch, if necessary. Now you get back, Mitsu."

The Japanese obeyed so swiftly that Tony scarcely knew when he was gone. He started along the path, almost reckless now whether the light of his torch should be seen by the fugitives.

But he was still some way from the landing-ground when the Bat taxied out of the hangar and took the air.

Tony began to run. He burst on to the landing-ground close to the hangar, took one look inside, and jumped for the governor switch. Every light went on immediately, and he was in a brilliant glare as he raced for his own Puss Moth.

It was a mad, reckless, magnificently courageous thing to do, this leaping into the night sky in pursuit of those criminal fugitives.

Yet it might have been that, despite the handicaps, Tony would have been able to pick up their direction and jockey them to a forced landing, for the Puss Moth was a very fast little machine.

But one thing the lad had overlooked. That was the fact that Liddle, Errol's trusted senior chauffeur-mechanic, was in league with Brady and had gone off with him.

Liddle was not the man to overlook possible danger, and he had guarded against immediate air pursuit by the simple expedient of draining Tony's petrol tank of almost all its fluid. He was too cunning to inflict some major injury upon the engine, for he did not know when Tony might take it into his head to come out to the landing-ground to see if the machine was all right, which would have meant discovery.

There was enough petrol to get Tony into the air and start him southward, but then there broke out a tell-tale coughing and spitting which told their own tale.

Tony had no option but to turn back and try to reach the landing-ground before being forced down to a crash.

He banked steeply, expecting each moment to hear the engine give a last splutter, for he had guessed the trouble. Had he been another couple of miles on his way disaster would surely have overtaken him.

As it was, he had just enough height to glide down to the inside of the edge of the landing-ground after the engine failed. He landed without injury to himself or the Puss Moth, but it was a close shave, and when he slid out of the cockpit he was almost as sore at Liddle for tampering with his machine, leaving him to risk a crash, as he was sick over their escape.

CHAPTER IX INSPECTOR BLAIN'S CASE

GRANT RUSHTON was just passing through the village of Hambleden when the Bat zoomed past overhead.

So suddenly had the racket burst upon the night that Rushton knew instinctively the 'plane must have come from Errol's private landing-ground, about four miles distant.

He had been driving at a good clip along the deserted country road, for he was anxious to get back to the Grange. But now he stepped even harder on the accelerator.

Another mile or so, and he heard a second machine above him. The first was now well out of sight and hearing, so he could listen, with practised ear, to the irregular functioning of the second.

It did not take him long to guess that this was the Puss Moth, and that whoever was in it was having trouble.

He stopped the car and got out. He saw the machine bank steeply and vanish back towards Fingest. Then he heard the engine stop entirely and, anxious and perturbed, he jumped back into the car and covered the remaining distance at over fifty.

He drove up to the front porch of the Grange just as Tony appeared in the glare of the headlight. The police-sergeant and the local constable were both out in the drive. Mitsu, his wet trousers changed for dry garments, was standing in the doorway, a picture of the attentive servant.

Within a few moments Rushton was in possession of what had occurred. It was impossible to keep it from the sergeant, who was at a loss what to do.

In view of what had happened and his care for Errol, Rushton did not choose to advise him other than to suggest that he had better get on the telephone to Henley and inform Inspector Blain what had occurred.

Tony had made no mention before the sergeant of Brady and Rushton also suppressed the fact that he was a factor in the escape. He left it to the sergeant to puzzle over the mystery of the maid going off with Liddle.

The sergeant would have detained Rushton to speak further, but Rushton waved him away curtly.

"I've got nothing to say to you, sergeant," he said. "Mr. Errol is my client, and he has been placed under arrest at Henley. So don't expect me to do anything for you. Wait until you see Inspector Blain. He will, no doubt, have a solution for all your problems."

Up in the sitting-room which they used jointly, Rushton heard in detail all that Tony could tell him. During their conversation Mitsu stole into the room to beg Rushton for news of his master.

Rushton at any time would have been considerate of the little Jap, for he knew how intensely loyal he was to his master. But now, in view of what he had done for Tony, he was particularly considerate.

Rising, he laid one hand on the valet's shoulder.

"Listen, Mitsu," he said in a low tone, "you have nothing to worry about. Mr. Errol will be released. I promise you that. I have made no protest at his arrest because I had hoped that it would enable me to catch the guilty persons napping. They have made a swift and unexpected move, and I never guessed that Liddle was one of them. But your master will be free before we finish with this affair."

Mitsu took his hand and bent over it in low salaam. Then he glided from the room like a shadow.

"This is the very devil of a complication, Tony," said Rushton when he had gone. "I should have thought of the possibility of Liddle or one of the other servants being in league with Brady. On the other hand, it is obvious that he was kept closely informed of all that went on in this house. Otherwise he could never have chosen the exact moment as he did. What we have to do now is to find where he has been lying low. This thing wasn't planned in a day or a week. It took months to lead up to the psychological moment. I've got a hunch where he may have been hanging out, and as soon as it is dawn—"

He broke off as the door opened again and Mitsu once more appeared. Approaching close, he looked at Rushton.

"Master," he breathed, "when Mitsu lay by bridge, he heard some things that man and woman said. If master wishes, Mitsu will tell."

"By all means, Mitsu. What was it?"

"Mitsu did not hear all, master, but Mitsu thinks man who went with maid was artist who has been living in old windmill on hill. Mitsu heard him speak of it. Woman asked if he would go back, and he said he would not go to trouble."

"By George," cried Tony, "I never thought of that. That's where the light was that I saw. I thought the artist was keeping mighty late hours."

"And that old windmill is exactly the place I was going to

investigate at dawn," finished Rushton. "You have given me just what I wanted, Mitsu. We shall go there."

"Dawn come quickly, now, master—half-hour, mebbe."

He was right. In half an hour the first grey tinge was showing in the east, and under the sombre, inquisitive eyes of the police-sergeant, Rushton and Tony set off in the chill air as if for a stroll.

They took the path that Tony had followed in the night. They came to the rustic bridge, which they crossed, and then, passing the summer-house came to the ring fence that separated that part of the estate from the road that ran up through the valley to Oxford.

It was no more than eight hundred yards from this point to the old windmill, where the four blades still hung in silhouette against the sky.

But the path up from the road was very steep.

They were a little out of breath when they arrived before the heavy old door.

Rushton did not waste time knocking. Already he had gone through a process of elimination regarding the possible places where Brady could have holed in during his time of preparing for the coup.

He knew it would have to be a place that was close to the Grange, would have to be of such a nature that Brady would have prefect freedom of action, and also one with which Brady would be able to identify himself in some character that would not cause comment.

For these reasons the usual village cottages could be eliminated. Likewise the local inn. He had heard that the windmill was occupied, and it had at once leaped to his mind, when he guessed that the killing of Carrie Richfield was due to an outside force, that this would be an ideal place as a base.

He did not expect to find much, but he was not there to search for a mass of evidence. Brady was too wily a bird to leave loose ends sticking out.

But he was keen on finding one thing if it remained there, for it needed just such an item to complete the chain of theory he had formed. And what Mitsu had told him gave him a slight hope that Brady might have gone in such a hurry as to leave this piece of evidence behind, not really caring now whether it were found or not.

The door yielded readily. They stepped into an octagonal-shaped room, the walls of which narrowed towards the ceiling with the slope of the tower.

The place was furnished very simply as a living-room and kitchen combined, there being an oil cooking-stove at one side. It was neat enough, with absolutely nothing to show that it might have been used by the notorious criminal, "Flash" Brady.

Access was gained to the next floor by a narrow spiral iron staircase, and this, after switching on his torch, Rushton began to climb, followed by Tony who had taken the precaution to pull out his gun.

They emerged into a somewhat smaller octagonal apartment that also narrowed towards the ceiling, and this they found to be furnished as a bedroom, its appointments being almost spartan. There was a small camp-bed, a chair, a washstand, a table—nothing else. Nor did they find anything to suggest Brady.

From here a ladder passed through a hole in the floor above. They climbed it, to find themselves in the top and smallest of the three rooms into which the tower had been divided.

There were four large windows, all of which gave on to a narrow gallery that ran right round the outside of the tower, and against one of them could be seen the dilapidated slats of one of the arms of the windmill.

This place was furnished as a studio, and all about were canvases in various stages of composition, as proof that the occupant was an artist.

There was all the other usual confusion of a studio, but, search though they might, they could discover no definite proof of Brady's occupancy.

Rushton was about to turn and lead the way down, when suddenly his attention was arrested by a half-finished landscape that stood on one of the easels.

It was not a particularly good piece of work. In fact, from a technical point of view it would have ranked very low indeed, so amateurish was it in the execution.

But something familiar about the subject held Rushton's frowning attention for some minutes. Then he slapped his thigh softly.

"Brady was here all right, Tony. Here is the proof."

"That thing, chief? Where is the proof?"

"Look at this picture carefully. Have you never seen that sugar-loaf mountain before? Don't you recognise something familiar about it? And the way that cliff descends so abruptly to terrific depths?"

Tony puzzled over it, but shook his head.

"It seems familiar, but I can't quite place it."

"Well, I can. It is in the Riff country in Morocco, in the very heart of the mountain district that was held by Abdel Krim for so long against the Spaniards and French. There's your proof, for no man could have a better recollection of that country than Brady."

"That's right! I recognise it now. It tells us Brady was here all right."

"And it tells us what was in his mind," added Rushton grimly.

When Rushton and Tony got back to the Grange they found both Major Holden, the Chief Constable of the county, and Inspector Blain.

The inspector had heard from the sergeant of the escape of the dead woman's maid in company with Liddle, and Major Holden had already got through to Scotland Yard to inform them of the fact, to give them a description of both the fugitives, and to ask that a general alarm be sent out.

He had no suspicion yet of the identity of the "maid," nor did he know anything about Brady, the most important factor in the case.

Major Holden greeted Rushton cordially. They had met many times, and he did not entertain the inexplicable antagonism which Inspector Blain had displayed.

"I am very sorry to hear this about Mark Errol," he said. "I have met him. It seems incredible that he could do such a thing. Still, one never knows when a skeleton will pop out of the cupboard."

"Errol never shot the woman," said Rushton quietly. "I should think the fact that the maid has taken flight would be proof enough that her statement was not to be relied upon."

"Someone is going to be hauled over the coals for allowing her to get away," snarled the inspector, with a glare at the luckless sergeant.

"Do you care to say anything, Rushton?" went on the Chief Constable, ignoring the inspector's outburst.

"When will you hold the inquest?"

"Dr. Green will be along any moment now. I stopped there on my way. He is also the coroner. I thought we would hold the inquest here at two o'clock this afternoon."

"I don't mind making a statement to you in strict privacy," said Rushton slowly, "but as I am acting professionally for Errol, I think I had better refrain from speaking fully until the inquest. At the same time, I cannot too strongly impress upon you the importance of capturing the fugitives. There were not two of them—there were three. And the third is, in my opinion, the person who murdered Mrs. Richfield."

"What on earth do you mean? I did not know there was anyone else missing."

The inspector and sergeant had stepped closer.

"No one from the house, major. I know the real identity of the maid. She is a criminal adventuress well known at Scotland Yard and to the police of other cities. But I shall say more later. This, I take it, is the doctor. If you will give me permission I should like to be in the room when he makes his report. I am anxious to see that bullet when it is found. I don't know if Inspector Blain has had time yet to make a thorough search."

"Isn't it still in the body?" asked Holden.

"No. It passed out beneath the lower ribs at the back. The woman was shot while sitting in the chair at the desk. She fell from that to the floor. I believe the bullet should be found somewhere beyond the end of the desk, between it and the bookcases. And I'd like to make a detailed examination of that pistol. I ask this as the one acting professionally for Errol."

Major Holden was amazed to hear that, if the bullet had passed right through the body, no extended search had yet been made for it. His manner was restrained and cool to the inspector, who, as soon as he could, took himself upstairs.

The others followed. The doctor's report was only what was to be expected. Death had been instantaneous, and due to some object, undoubtedly a bullet, passing clean through the heart. He showed that it had emerged just as Rushton surmised.

During this examination the inspector was conducting a search for the bullet. He found it lying on the carpet just under one end of the desk. There were marks along the base of the bookcase which had been caused by the bullet ricochetting after emerging from the dead woman's body.

Rushton asked to see it, and, with his pocket-glass, made a careful study of it. He made no comment, however, when he handed it back to Inspector Blain.

He next managed to get possession of the pistol, and, with Holden looking on, exhibited its present loading and condition. He had been holding it with a handkerchief in his hand, and now he passed it back. But again he made no comment as to whether this was important to him or not.

It was definitely decided to hold the inquest that afternoon, and for the purpose the big dining-room at the Grange was to be turned into a coroner's court.

Quite unperturbed by the upheaval in the house, Mrs. Dean had breakfast ready at eight o'clock, sufficient for twice the number who were to partake of it.

In Errol's absence, Rushton was, for the time being, acting as host, though he left nearly everything to Mrs. Dean and Mitsu.

After breakfast he had a talk with Major Holden. He knew that the Chief Constable was finding himself in a somewhat difficult position between him and Inspector Blain, for it was growing more and more evident that Blain was in entire disagreement with Rushton's participation in the case.

But Rushton wasn't worrying on that score, now that he was acting officially for Mark Errol.

He feared, however, that he might encounter strong antagonism at the inquest to the theory he proposed advancing, and realised, too, that even to Major Holden, who appreciated his methods of work, it might come as no little surprise, so startling was it.

He made mention of his strong belief in Errol's innocence, by way of opening.

"If you know something that will prove his innocence, then why did you permit him to be taken along without protest?" was a natural question on Holden's part.

Rushton nodded.

"I can understand how you feel about that. I will tell you. As I have said, I recognised the 'maid' as a well-known criminal adventuress with whom I have had some passages at arms in the past. Her name is Gloria Ravissa."

"Good heavens! You don't say so? I have read about that woman. Wasn't she an actress?"

"A dancer. And, of course, you know about the notorious crook, 'Flash' Brady—an ex-inspector of Scotland Yard?"

"Of course. Do you mean to say he is mixed up in this?"

"I am certain he was. I only suspected it yesterday, but now I have what I consider absolute proof. Look here, major, I am going to make a full statement to you of the case I propose advancing at the inquest. I do not know what line Blain will take, but I have a hunch that he is already committed to his own theory, and that it bodes no good for my client. But I want you to understand the things that I have found and how I link them up."

"I shall be more than interested to hear."

"Mind you, I haven't yet got the chief exhibit which I shall need if my theory is to be proved as iron-clad fact. That, unfortunately, is missing. And so is the chief witness in the affair, who, to my mind, should be in the dock. That is Brady, and the exhibit is a weapon of .25 calibre—I am not prepared to state definitely whether that weapon is a rifle or pistol, but I am strongly inclined to think it is a high-powered rifle."

"But the weapon that was found?"

"I shall come to that. Let us begin at the beginning."

He filled and lit his pipe and took a turn up and down the dining-room before continuing.

"This crime consists of two parts," he went on. "There is the first part, which covers the blackmailing of Mark Errol for a large sum of money. The second part is the murder of Mrs. Richfield. You already know her history, and how she came to England to blackmail her former husband over their son. Well, thank goodness, the son is safe enough now.

"But there was another plot, and a deeper one, of which, I am convinced, neither Mrs. Richfield nor her husband had an inkling. They were only cat's-paws in the hands of 'Flash' Brady and Gloria Ravissa."

"You believe Richfield innocent?"

"He is guilty of being a party to the blackmail, and his New York record is bad, very bad. But I am convinced he had no part in the murder of his wife."

"I'll bear that in mind."

"We haven't got the full facts yet, but it is plain that Brady met the Richfields in New York, learned what they were planning, and took charge of the whole thing. He installed his partner, Gloria Ravissa, as maid to Mrs. Richfield, and thus was kept in contact with them while he was elaborating things here. He came to England in order to be on the ground. He came down here and took over that old converted windmill, posing as an artist. From there he could keep a constant surveillance upon Errol. But that didn't put him inside the house. So, in order to manage that difficulty, he arranged that Errol's senior chauffeur-mechanic should fall ill, and that his own man, Liddle, should get the place."

"A masterly plot—if you are right."

"It was; and before I finish I shall prove it. But the rest was more so. Through Liddle he could keep tabs of everything, and direct certain arrangements, if necessary. He was all set when the Richfields arrived to put through the blackmailing stunt. The Richfields believed that the blackmailing stunt was the beginning and end of the affair. Brady had different ideas. The murder of Mrs. Richfield, with Richfield being dragged in in some way, and suspicion thrown definitely upon Errol, was the masterpiece he evolved. And he pulled it off.

"He knew, of course, that Mrs. Richfield possessed a .25 calibre revolver. It was easy enough for him to provide himself with a high-powered weapon of the same calibre. Now you may ask how could Brady know the psychological moment at which to shoot. All the conditions had to be just so. Well, he undoubtedly had several plans, but this one could be aided by an accomplice who was inside the house and close to Mrs. Richfield. That accomplice was his partner—Gloria Ravissa."

"Your theory is at least interesting."

"A word from Gloria Ravissa to her mistress would ensure that she insisted on seeing Errol alone. Brady would already know through Liddle that the study upstairs was the room in which Errol transacted all his private business, and the one which he was almost certain to choose for his interview with Mrs. Richfield. Gloria Ravissa had prepared the way by opening the french windows, leaving a clear way into the room and a clear view for anyone perched in one of the big leafy trees outside. That is where Brady was waiting."

"Good heavens!"

"I have no proof. That is again only theory. Then what happened? Errol and Mrs. Richfield came in. From where he sat Brady could see the business transacted. He saw Errol go to his safe and take out the bundle of bonds. He saw Mrs. Richfield sign the paper and take the bonds. Gloria Ravissa was outside on the balcony, also waiting. Then Brady saw Errol leave the room to fetch me as a witness to the document. It was then that Brady fired the fatal shot. We heard a muffled sound. Because we found a gun on the floor beside the dead woman it was a natural thing to jump to the conclusion that this was the weapon used. And, to strengthen the impression, we have the fact that the bullet found on the carpet is the size used by that pistol, that a single empty cartridge-case was found in the chamber in line with the barrel, while all the other chambers were filled with loaded cartridges, and that the barrel was fouled by a discharge. It is little wonder that Inspector Blain did not look farther."

"Nor should I. And I cannot understand why you insist that this other weapon was used."

"I will tell you. It is because there was one feature about the freshly discharged pistol which his revolver did not provide, and which Inspector Blain failed to notice."

"What was it?"

"The weapon was completely cold."

"Good heavens! It would have been hot, of course. Are you certain of this?"

"Absolutely."

Rushton explained how Richfield had grabbed up the weapon in accusing Errol of the murder, and how he had found it cold in taking it away from him.

"The gun was prepared," he went on. "As soon as Brady fired the shot from the tree—it was impossible for us to tell in the lounge just where the sound was located, and we took it for granted after seeing the study that it had been fired inside those walls—Gloria Ravissa rushed into the room, took the gun from Mrs. Richfield's bag, dropped it on the floor, grabbed the bundle of bonds, and rushed back through the window, pausing only long enough to fling the bonds out to the waiting Brady. She had just time to pass through the other room and gain the hall in time to see Errol, and it was easy enough for her to throw acute suspicion upon him by telling Blain that he was going away from the study instead of returning to it."

"This is one of the most extraordinary things I have ever heard."

"It is one of the best-arranged crimes I have ever been up against," returned Rushton.

"Then you believe Errol's statement?"

"I believe it completely."

"It is a pity Inspector Bain does not share that theory."

"Blain is going on the actual evidence of his own eyes. He is convinced that Errol did the shooting. Had I known earlier that Brady was to become a factor in my investigations, I should have strongly opposed Errol's arrest."

"Your theory sounds convincing to me, Rushton. But I don't know how it will go at the inquest."

"I am hopeful that I may convince Blain."

"There is one weak spot."

"I know. You mean that I cannot produce the other weapon which I maintain was used."

"Yes."

"Brady has either got rid of it effectually, or has taken it with him. But the end is not yet. I should be already in pursuit, were it not that my first duty is here. I must see Errol released."

Major Holden was inclined to agree with Rushton's theory, but his instinct was good in thinking it would not carry so much weight at the inquest as the police theory, if the latter were put emphatically.

And it was.

As a matter of fact, by that time Inspector Blain had become definitely hostile to Rushton. Whether it was the incident about the pistol or something else, one could not say, but his evidence was devastating.

Rushton took the stand first, and, in quiet, conversational tones, outlined the theory he had formed, bringing up each item in confirmation as he went along.

There was not the slightest doubt that he was making a very strong impression upon his hearers, with the exception of Inspector Bain, who sat gnawing at his moustache impatiently, and the sergeant, who took his colour from his superior.

By the time Rushton sat down he felt satisfied that he had assured the immediate release of Mark Errol. But, before Inspector Blain finished, he was flabbergasted to see the complete reversal of the atmosphere.

Blain made his case the stronger by a good-natured tolerance of Rushton's theory.

"We all know how clever and successful Mr. Grant Rushton has been," he said, "and I am sure none respect his abilities more than each man of the police. But I think, on this occasion, Mr. Rushton has allowed himself to rise into, shall we say, romance? His theory is a very pretty one and would make an excellent thriller story. But we are dealing with facts, gentlemen. And those facts are indisputable."

Then he laid down his points, one by one, with slow, telling emphasis. Bit by bit he built up a case that, angry though he was, Rushton had to confess sounded very convincing.

When Bain came to the matter of the pistol, he dismissed it with another tolerant smile.

"I don't think we need put too much stress on that," he said. "We all know that each person there was excited by what had occurred. Is it not possible that Mr. Rushton only thought afterwards about the temperature of the metal, that he told himself it was cold when, in reality, it had been warm? Remember only one shot had been fired, and some little time had elapsed before he and the others reached the room. The great indication of guilt, in the minds of the police, is the strong motive possessed by Mark Errol. No one had anything like such a motive. He was there, or very close to the spot when the shot was fired. And all the evidence goes to show that it was his hand that held the weapon.

"As for this suggestion that the notorious criminal 'Flash' Brady did the deed—I cannot see how that can be sustained. Is it likely that a criminal like Brady was living in the neighbourhood for many months planning just such a crime as this? Is it possible that he could have anticipated every small occurrence in order to lead up to such a crime and perform it at the psychological moment? I think it entirely outside the bounds of possibility, and as for a second weapon—well, as I said, a very pretty theory for a thriller."

He needed to say no more. His words utterly demolished the theory Rushton had put forward, and of course the weakest link in it all was the fact that Rushton could produce no such weapon as the second one he maintained had been used.

Nevertheless, he was aghast when Mark Errol was remanded on the definite charge of murder, and at the brief interview which he was granted he could give him little comfort.

"I had no idea Blain would take such a strong line," he told Errol. "But do not get downhearted. In his anxiety to make his case he has revealed the one brick in the edifice which will demolish the whole structure."

"I can't see any," muttered Errol gloomily.

"It is the second weapon. We've got to find that wherever it may be. Once I can produce that I can smash his case to smithereens."

"But how?"

"Ballistics. It is a well-known fact among gun experts that every barrel rifling of pistol or revolver leaves certain definite marks upon every bullet passing through it. We have the bullet that killed Mrs. Richfield. That bullet will retain certain marks visible under a microscope. Those marks must coincide with other peculiarities in the rifling of the weapon used. If I can produce that weapon and prove that the marks on the bullet could only have been made by that rifling, and that rifling only, then we've got the case in our pocket."

But Rushton was by no means as confident as he tried to make Errol believe.

He knew how easy it would be for Brady to dispose of such a weapon, and, in the absence of absolute proof such as he had indicated, he knew he could not convince a jury.

But he was determined to exert himself as never before in this challenge that had been thrown down, and his first care was to set Tony to work to try and locate the progress of such a plane as the one in which Brady had escaped.

Tony knew all the ropes of this sort of inquiry. He put through half a dozen different calls, and that evening was called back by the Air Advice Office at Croydon.

They passed on a report from Bordeaux that a Bat machine had passed over Bordeaux Aerodrome just after mid-day. She was heading south, possibly towards Biarritz or San Sebastian. At any rate her course seemed to be laid towards Spain.

That was enough to decide Rushton.

That same night they got away in Tony's Moth.

CHAPTER X   THE SPANISH BANDIT

BRADY was elated with the success of his coup.

By his double-crossing he had been able to net half a million, which was now all in his hands. And he had got rid of his accomplices. Under his original plan he would have had to share three-quarters of a million with the Richfields. And even then there would certainly have been complications. So Brady was very pleased with himself.

Moreover, he felt confident that he had left behind him a nut that not even Grant Rushton would crack for some little time. It didn't worry him very much if the truth did eventually come out about the murder of Carrie Richfield. He would be well away by then. But he figured that the condition in which things had been left would tie up Errol in a knot that he would find extremely difficult to unravel, and, privily, Brady thought there was quite a good chance that the stigma would remain with Errol even if he slid out of an actual charge of murder owing to insufficient evidence to convict. He did not know that Grant Rushton had handled the pistol while it should have been still warm.

And, on that, with Rushton's recognition of Gloria Ravissa rested the whole chance of success of the plot.

Nevertheless, Brady's getaway was as smooth as he could have wished. Liddle had done his work well. He did not know if Tony had crashed or not; he hoped he had.

But he did not know that they zoomed south at a nice cruising speed of eighty miles an hour, and told himself with a grin that, while they were looking down upon the moon-washed English Channel, chaos must reign back at Fingest Grange.

He could not have pulled off the thing had he not built his plot carefully and patiently around each individual item that touched Mark Errol.

The keynote had been the kidnapped child. Then the Richfields, and, finally, his own ability to apply those factors to Errol's own intense desire to get possession of his son.

The whole thing had been nearly wrecked summarily when Bryant Kennedy succeeded in getting possession of the boy, but Brady had made such a swift contra move that he had caught Kennedy napping.

For months he had matured his plans patiently. Gloria Ravissa was, of course, invaluable. The Richfields were mere ciphers in his plot. But without Gloria Ravissa as an inside accomplice he could not have timed things to the exact point. Nor without Liddle could he have managed such a perfect getaway.

Proof of how exactly he had timed everything was the fact that despite the actual presence of Grant Rushton and Tony in the house, he had carried it off just the same.

Nor had Brady planned only so far as the actual completion of matters at Fingest Grange and the getaway. Long experience had told him that if he were to enjoy the fruits of victory, he must prepare the way after.

There were the bonds to cash. That would not be difficult. He had hoped for actual cash, but, after all, bearer bonds were better even than banknotes of large denomination. Any responsible bank or banker must accept them, and he didn't mind if he had to accept something under their face value.

But safety from pursuit—to ensure that he could disregard discovery no matter how soon it might come, that was his aim. And he believed he had succeeded.

While he was still in New York, and when he was first working out the details of his scheme, he had borne this in mind with the result that after canvassing all the possibilities—there were plenty—he decided to get into touch with a certain man in Spain.

This individual was one whom Brady had known in the time when, as Sakr-el-Droog or "Hawk of the Peak," he had been confidant and chief captain to Abdel Krim, the Lion of the Riff in Morocco, that doughty fighter who had kept the Spaniards at bay for well on two years and only succumbed when the French took a hand as well.

Count Larida, the one in question, had carried on an extensive business in the smuggling of arms from certain European ports into the Riff country. He had made a huge fortune at the time, but, like so many gamblers who win in one way, he lost in another.

Born in Catalonia, he was, first, last and always, a Catalonian, and whichever Government ruled Spain, royalist or republican, he was against it.

He would never rest content until Catalonia was independent and Barcelona acknowledged as its capital. Any Spanish Government regarded this as a traitorous proposal, but, even in the days when

Larida was smuggling arms into the Riff to one of Spain's most obstinate enemies, the most cunning of the Government scouts had found it impossible to get sufficient evidence against him to convict him, although they knew that he was in the thing up to his neck.

With the passing of the monarchy in Spain, and the coming of the republic, Larida redoubled his efforts to secure the independence of Catalonia. He would have nothing to do even with the orthodox party, that would have secured this independence by constitutional means. Nor would he have any truck with the Communists, who would have secured the same end by direct action.

He lived in a semi-fortress not far out of Barcelona, and from here he directed the activities of his own small but dangerous party, whose policy was independence of Catalonia under Larida as its first President.

He had no intention that the Communists should take over the banks and spread the money among themselves. He intended those plums for himself, for he was no true patriot. He was a super-bandit who, nevertheless, had spent almost all his vast fortune made from smuggling arms and other illicit means in furthering his plans.

At the time when he received a letter from Brady, he was living a life of enforced quiet. Most of his money was gone, and the orthodox party in Catalonia seemed to be too strong for him.

Therefore, when Brady hinted that he might have something worth while to put up to him, he had jumped at the suggestion, and later, when Brady had asked if sanctuary would be available, he had offered him the use of his fortress-like estate and all within it.

This, then, was Brady's destination after making his getaway from Fingest Grange.

A night landing at the place would have been impossible. Although the estate itself stood on a miniature plateau or shelf, half-way up the range of mountains—the Sierra de Lallena, some fifty miles west of Barcelona—it was by no means easy of access by 'plane even in daylight, and, until the landing-ground was equipped with brilliant guide-lights, not even an expert pilot like Liddle could have succeeded in coming down safely.

Moreover, there were many choppy air-currents continually pouring up the valley, with treacherous pockets into which a machine might plunge without warning to a crash in the boulder-strewn bed of one of the numerous streams that drained the range.

The landing, however, was timed nicely for late in the afternoon. The Pyrenees were crossed almost directly above the tiny independent state of Andorra, then Liddle followed the valley of the Segre River until they could see the first jutting points of the Sierra de Lallena.

It was not, however, until the 'plane had swung round the northern nose of the mountains, and had covered some farther miles along the eastern slopes, that Brady spotted the *residencia* which was their destination.

It was set in a most isolated position in the centre of a wooden plateau. From above, it seemed that mountains hemmed it in on every side.

Immediately surrounding the house the ground had been cleared away, and from above it could be seen that the roof-area was very extensive.

Far beneath were many little mountain streams, tumbling along rocky beds, and so eager were they in their course that one could almost imagine the sound of their hoarse rumblings, though, of course, that was impossible through the roar of the engine.

Over the mountains was a cold, almost steely blue in which clouds were forming in quick sequence only to be torn to tatters and shreds by the conflicting winds that blew from every direction.

The *residencia* or mansion grew even larger upon closer approach, and then those in the 'plane could see two bastion-like towers at each front corner, the slit-like apertures in the old stone commanding a view of the only possible approach up the valley.

They saw, too, that the lower storey was completely without windows. There were only the same sort of slits as had been pierced in the bastions, making of the building a fortress that would be most difficult to capture even in these days of bombing 'planes and modern artillery.

But what Brady and Liddle sought most was the landing-ground. In front of the house a flat square could be seen, but this was patterned with green which on closer acquaintance would have been seen to consist of pomegranate trees and vines.

There were also flat, open spaces on the other three sides, but nothing indicative of a landing-ground, and both Brady and Liddle were beginning to get anxious on that point when, suddenly, Gloria Ravissa caught Brady's arm and pointed.

He followed the direction of her arm, and saw that she was

pointing towards the roof. He saw a man dancing about, waving his arms in frantic signal, and then swinging each hand down towards the roof.

Brady read his meaning, and touched Liddle. The aviator had already taken notice, and Brady could see him shaking his head. Nevertheless, he banked steeply, and brought the machine round so that he was approaching the house directly from the north. All the time he was sliding down through the tricky pockets of air until, when he zoomed over the roof, he was less than fifty feet above it.

Now they could see clearly just what was meant. The roof itself was perfectly flat, and, with this as a basis, it had not been difficult to turn it into a small landing-ground, larger, it is true, than the deck-space of a modern seaplane-carrier, but tricky enough at that.

The man beneath had stopped waving and was watching. Brady had just time to recognise him as Count Larida when the roof vanished and Liddle was banking steeply once more.

For the second time he brought the machine round to the north side of the house, and now, in the way in which he manoeuvred, they saw he was going to try for a landing.

He shut off his engine at what seemed a reckless moment; but, whatever his moral calibre, Liddle certainly knew his job. He slid in over the edge of the roof at almost falling speed, the wheels touched, left purchase, and touched again. Then the 'plane ran along the roof until it encountered a belt of rope that yielded firmly but surely to the impact. Liddle was braking gently all the time, and when the 'plane at last came to rest, there was still more than thirty feet between him and the south end of the roof.

Count Larida rushed to the side to greet them. He broke into voluble Spanish and English mixed, and assisted Gloria Ravissa to alight.

Looking him over, Brady thought he had altered a great deal since he had last seen him. Previously he had been stout, short and of a certain devil-may-care manner. Now he was much thinner, lacked his former *sangfroid* of manner, and, it was obvious to Brady, found it no easy matter to appear lighthearted.

"Larida has been through something," was what Brady thought.

He was to learn before long a little of what that was, and when he did, even his hard-bitten nature was to recoil with horror.

They descended from the roof by means of a trapdoor. The old stone staircase was enclosed by walls right down to the bottom, where they stepped out on to a pillared gallery that must have been very beautiful before the place had been allowed to deteriorate.

Count Larida turned to the right and conducted them along this gallery, and Brady noticed that they passed three other enclosed staircases as they went. This meant that the mansion was divided into several separate sections, each section forming a distinct unit by itself.

Beneath the gallery was the green, open space they had seen from the 'plane, and now, at close view, they could distinguish a mass of brightly-coloured flowers set among the pomegranates, though the whole patio had a look of neglect.

Larida was just about to lead them through some broad French windows into a big salon, when the party was halted by the sudden appearance of a woman on the gallery ahead of them.

She had appeared, Brady guessed, either through another French window, or down one of the enclosed staircases, reaching that from one of the numerous doors that opened on to each.

She made a striking figure as she stood, dark of hue, exquisite of form and feature, and slumbrous of eye. She was dressed in yellow as vivid as ripe lemon; her hair, very black, was gathered in a huge coil at the back, and in the coils was a warm yellow rose.

Brady noticed an immediate change in his host.

He saw him stiffen and moved ahead like a panther. He and Gloria Ravissa and Liddle still remained behind, for they believed this must be the Countess Larida, and certainly her attitude did not appear to be that of one who was about to extend a warm welcome.

The woman was standing like a statue, her bosom heaving tumultuously, as though she were suppressing some strong emotion. But her eyes were not on Larida, nor on Brady or Liddle. They were fixed upon Gloria Ravissa.

Larida was almost upon her before she paid him any attention. The others could hear him saying something in low, hurried words, but could not distinguish what it was.

The woman brought her gaze round to him, and then there flashed in her face such an expression of anger, abhorrence and contempt mixed, that it revealed her as the incarnation of fury suppressed.

With a swift movement she turned and vanished through the opening from which she had emerged, and Larida paused.

He turned back with a shrug, but Brady saw that the sweat was standing on his forehead and that his face had gone a sickly grey.

"Things don't look too pleasant," he murmured swiftly to Gloria Ravissa.

"The woman is a tigress, and I believe I am the cause," she returned.

But there was time for no more, for Larida was inviting them into the salon.

The apartment was huge, magnificent in its heyday, but now only the dilapidated ghost of what it had once been.

The plastered walls were cracked; the exquisite figuring of the gesso broken, the moulded plaster of the ceiling stained and chipped away in great blobs.

Dingy but valuable paintings were on the walls and silken hangings that had come out of the East centuries ago hung in decay. The carpets still held their pristine colours, but these were marred with worn and ugly stains.

The furniture was heavy old carved Spanish mahogany, upholstered with brocades that had faded long ago. The huge glass chandelier that hung from the centre of the ceiling, and had seen many a gallant gathering in the past, was fly-specked, broken, and crusted in layers of dust.

It was a depressing apartment as it stood.

On the mahogany centre table were decanters of sherry and port, with a bottle of Scotch whisky, a siphon and glasses. There were biscuits and Spanish cigarettes.

Larida invited his guests to be seated, and himself passed round the wine and whisky. He did not speak until Gloria Ravissa had taken a glass of the old brown sherry and Brady had poured out a generous measure of whisky for himself and Liddle. Larida took a small glass of sherry with Gloria Ravissa.

He toasted them with a bow and then said suavely:

"Senora la contessa does not enjoy good health, so I hope that you will forgive her not being here to receive you."

Gloria Ravissa murmured some polite nothing, while Brady nodded genially enough.

"We understand, *amigo*. It is enough that you were here and that we receive your hospitality. I am ready to explain the business whenever you wish it."

Larida glanced at Liddle and Gloria Ravissa, but Brady made a gesture with his hand.

"We're all in this, *amigo*. And the sooner you understand what I want, the better."

"I am ready whenever you wish to speak," said Larida in quite good English.

"How are things with you?"

"They do not advance as well as could be."

"Are you in retreat here, or are you at liberty to go into Barcelona?"

"I do not go into Barcelona at the moment personally, but I have trustworthy connection with the city."

"You'd better throw all this and come across to the Riff with me, *amigo.*"

"It is impossible."

From the way he spoke, Brady knew that he did not wish to make any confidences in front of Liddle and Gloria Ravissa. But he could guess that Larida was in a bad way, though whether it was through politics, money, his wife, or all three combined, he did not know yet.

"Well, *amigo,*" he went on coolly, "we've pulled off a pretty good thing in England, and it is absolutely necessary that we lie low for a bit. After that, I am thinking of going across to the Riff. Once there, I can defy the world."

"You are welcome, as you know, to whatever hospitality and protection I can give you, my friend. I do not forget the past. But just now I am not in a position to do much."

"You mean financially?"

"Financially and politically."

"You won't have any immediate need to worry about money if you come in with me. I want some transactions put through in Barcelona. It will take a few days, and can be done quite openly—no risk to you. There will be a million pesetas in it for you— about twenty-five thousand pounds."

Larida's eyes brightened.

"That would be very welcome."

"Very well. This evening I will go into full details with you."

Larida rose.

"With your permission I shall call a woman servant to show Senorita Gloria Ravissa to her room. I will take you and Senor Liddle myself."

He disappeared, to return with a buxom Spanish girl, who took Gloria Ravissa in charge. Standing on the gallery, Brady saw that they disappeared into one of the enclosed staircases which they had passed after descending from the roof.

Larida led him and Liddle along to the next one and, after mounting about half-way, opened a door on the right. He ushered Brady into this room and, opening a door exactly opposite, indicated that the room was Liddle's.

He returned to Brady.

"We shall dine in half an hour in the salon where we have been talking," he said. "I am sorry that conditions here are not quite normal. But to you, *amigo,* I must tell the truth. You saw the senora on the gallery?"

"Yes."

"That was the Countess Larida."

"I did not know you had married."

"Two years ago. It was an unlucky day for me. I will be frank. This *residencia* was hers. What madness prompted me to marry, I do not know. But since that day my life has been a nightmare, *amigo.* She is not normal; she is consumed with a madness of jealousy—of me, of my speech with any other person, even the local padre. When she knew you were coming, and that a lady would be of the party, she went into one of her frenzies. It was the worst yet. I thought you had better know."

"I am glad you told me this. I thought something was wrong when I saw her on the gallery. Senorita Gloria Ravissa guessed correctly. Is she— is there any danger for the senorita?"

"I do not think so, but it will be as well if she locks her door to-night."

"I'll tell her. Look here, Larida, while we are alone, perhaps I'd better tell you what I want you to arrange."

"If you care to do so."

Brady told him about the coup he had pulled off at Fingest Grange in England, and described the nature of the bearer bonds which formed the prize.

"There is no danger to you in getting cash against them," he went on. "There can be no possible come-back. They can't be refused in England, and they can't stop payment against them. The only string is that if they are able to trace the bank through which they were cashed, then they might pass that clue on to Grant Rushton."

"Grant Rushton—the English detective."

"Yes, and the one man I'd like to finish off!" snarled Brady. "I won't bother to explain now, but he knows it was I who pulled off this thing. He'll try to follow it up."

"So you will want me to make haste."

"Yes. Can you start things to-morrow?"

"It is Sunday."

"I'd forgotten. Monday, then."

"I will make all arrangements. How much is the total?"

"Half a million pounds."

"Twenty million pesetas! That is a great sum to arrange in one transaction."

"Make it in more transactions, then."

"And influence?"

"I'll pay for it. And don't forget that I am giving you a clean million for yourself."

"I need it. Believe me, *amigo,* I'd give more than that sum if I could get away from here and go across to Morocco."

"Well, why can't you?"

"It is my wife. It was because I regarded this place as an ideal fortress in case of trouble that I was influenced to marry her. I did not know that she was insane upon one point. And she was pretty enough. But it has been terrible, *amigo*—terrible!"

"I'd tame her," said Brady with a grin. "Take a rawhide whip to her, Larida."

What reply Larida might have made was stopped by a terrific outburst in some other part of the house. It was completely inhuman, as if some animal were being tortured beyond endurance.

It was uncanny to hear the sounds, rising into screams of savage rage, and then dying down into pitiful moans. Brady stood transfixed, staring at Larida. Larida had gone as grey as dust, his jaw was hanging loose, his whole body was shaking as if in an ague.

Still the terrible cries continued, rising to such a pitch of dementia that even Brady felt the horror of it.

Liddle came rushing in without ceremony, his eyes popping from his head. It was due to his opening of the door that the screams reached them even more clearly and admitted another sound which

Brady recognised plainly enough.

This was the voice of Gloria Ravissa, raised in a shrill call for help. Larida broke into action as if released from a steel spring. He shot out to the stairs and went down them at a rush.

Brady and Liddle followed. They landed on to the gallery and saw Larida running like one beset by devils towards the right end. They took after him, and Brady's long legs lengthened their stride as, once more, he heard Gloria Ravissa scream for help.

Larida vanished into the enclosed staircase that led to Gloria's apartment. Brady and Liddle took after him. But, even as they did so, a fresh noise rose sharp and clear above the wild screaming above. It was the explosion of a pistol. And, with it, all sound died.

They arrived at Gloria's door and found it open. They saw Gloria standing by the bed, holding her right arm just above the wrist. On the floor at her feet was the body of Countess Larida. In the front of her yellow dress was a deep stain that was already welling on to the floor. Brady needed but one look to know that she had been shot clean through the heart, and on the floor beside her was Gloria Ravissa's pearl-handled automatic pistol.

It was Brady who reached Gloria first.

"What was it?" he asked sharply.

She swayed on her feet. Then she held up her wrist so that he could see. It had been bitten clean through to the bone, just as if some wild animal had leaped upon her. But he knew whose teeth had been buried there.

"That she-devil," he muttered. "Come over here until I bathe it. Get up to my room, Liddle, and get my first-aid kit."

While he bathed the wound the girl told him what had occurred. Neither knew that Larida was standing close, listening to every word.

"I did not know she was in the room until I heard a noise and turned round," she said with an effort. "I smiled at her and began to speak, but she only moved towards me silently. Her eyes were strange, and I felt that something was wrong. Then she put out her hand as if she wanted to take mine, and I gave it to her, thinking that perhaps she wanted to make up for her rudeness on our arrival.

"But the moment she got hold of my fingers she acted like one demented. She gave a cry like an animal and jerked me towards her. She bent her head and fastened her teeth in my wrist and then began to chew at the flesh like an animal. It was dreadful. I managed to drag my arm away, and then she burst into the most awful cries. I fought her off as best I could, but she had the strength of a dozen, and I knew I was doomed unless help came.

"I screamed, but did not know if I would be heard. I tried to reach the door, but she was too quick for me. And then she caught me again close to the bed. I had already put my pistol under the pillow. I fought her off in desperation until I could get hold of it. My right hand was almost paralysed from the mauling her teeth had given it, but I managed to get the pistol out and up between us. She saw it and drew back, and then she came on again and I—fired. I think I have killed her."

"And a good job, too," murmured Brady, not realising that Larida was so close.

"A sentiment which I endorse, *amigo,*" came Larida's voice. "I ask you to look?"

Brady turned to see Larida drawing up his sleeve to reveal a great jagged scar in the left forearm.

"That was done while I slept, *amigo.* I only awoke in time. Senorita has nothing to fear. No one outside this house shall know how this has happened. And," he added with a sudden change to his whole countenance, "this means that I shall be able to come to the Riff with you, *amigo.*"

He turned and regarded the body unemotionally.

"As soon as you have bandaged the senorita's arm I shall show her to another chamber. Then I will send for my friend, the local padre, who knows how things have been. Later to-night we shall dispose of this."

With that the cold-blooded little wretch left the room, walking as jauntily as if he had received some very pleasant news, which, indeed, he had.

CHAPTER XI   RUSHTON ON THE SCENT

It was not through Croydon that Grant Rushton got his first definite news of the Bat, but from the A.A. (Automobile Association) private wireless report station at Heston.

As a member of that body as well as of the R.A.C. he had put through urgent inquiries, and it was through the A.A. that he received a definite series of reports

Using the original information from Croydon as a base on which to work, they had followed the Bat with certainty as far as Toulouse. But there the trail practically ended.

The report from Toulouse was positive enough that a 'plane answering to the description of the one in question had crossed Toulouse at an hour that would fit in with her passing over Bordeaux; and it was equally positive that it was heading almost due south.

But from that point there was nothing. If the report were correct, then there were several points towards which she might be bound. Barcelona lay in a direct line from Toulouse, but that direction might only have been assumed to baffle any observers.

Similarly, she might turn more easterly and make for Marseilles. On the other hand, if she turned westerly she would fetch Madrid, or, varying direction a little here and there, she might make for one of a dozen different places in Spain, France, or Portugal.

The one positive thing was that, after the limit of her cruising distance, she would be forced to come down somewhere for petrol.

In anticipation of this, Rushton had notification sent broadcast for a watch to be kept for such a machine, and as he could do nothing about pursuit until he had some definite clue, there was no chance of making a further move for the moment.

Sunday passed without any further information coming in. On Monday Rushton went into the City and gave full particulars about the bonds which had been stolen.

His plan was comprehensive, for it covered every bank with foreign branches, agencies, and correspondents. In each case no difficulty was made about telegrams being sent broadcast throughout France, Spain, Portugal, and Italy. He even had special telegrams sent to Tangier, Casablanca, Oran, and Algiers, for he was remembering Brady's former close connection with Morocco, and had a strong suspicion that he might make for the security of the Riff. But he would be unable to negotiate any bonds in the Riff, where no banks existed. If he tried to dispose of them along the coast of North Africa, it would almost certainly be at one of the places mentioned.

These efforts brought quicker results than he expected. While nothing further arrived about the Bat, Rushton was called on the 'phone just before midday Tuesday by the manager of the Anglo-Spanish Bank and asked to come to the bank as soon as possible.

Tony drove him to the City in the Grey Panther, and as soon as he was in the manager's private room that individual handed him a decoded telegram. It ran as follows:

"Three banks in Barcelona have cashed in British Government Bearer Bonds, Series 8X5432,-7, to total amount of four hundred thousand pounds, at discount of fifteen per cent. Encashment performed through well-known Catalonian political leader. Advise if we are to take any steps."

"That is something to go on," said Rushton as he laid the paper down. "I am deeply grateful to you, Mr. Barnes."

"We are glad to oblige you, Mr. Rushton. What do you wish us to do now?"

"I hardly know what to say. Those bonds, as I told you, were stolen. The banks which cashed them in cannot lose any money. The fact though that the person who negotiated them was willing to accept fifteen per cent. discount on bonds that are quoted at par, should have made them suspicious that something was wrong. I shall have to go to Barcelona at once. I wonder if you would be kind enough to give me a letter of introduction to your correspondent there?"

"Of course, with the greatest pleasure. I shall write one at once."

Rushton and Tony took the journey in two stages. They stopped overnight at Le Bourget, but early on Wednesday morning were off again from Paris.

Taking a more direct route than that followed by Brady, and cruising at about the same speed, Tony had Perpignan on the Gulf of Lyons beneath them at about half-past eleven, by midday they were across the eastern spur of the Pyrenees, and at almost precisely one o'clock in the afternoon he set the Moth down on the municipal aerodrome at Barcelona—a smooth, punctual, uneventful journey.

They motored into the city almost at once, where Rushton visited the bank and presented his letter of credence.

He was received by the manager who, although born in

Barcelona and a Spanish or, rather, Catalonian citizen, was half English, his mother having been the daughter of an English banker.

He had received a portion of his education in England, and through his present position was in close touch with English affairs. He knew all about Grant Rushton, and received him cordially.

"What is the trouble about those bonds, Mr. Rushton?" he asked as soon as Rushton was seated.

"The bonds, in themselves, are perfectly all right and as sound as the British Government," responded Rushton. "But," he added bluntly, "the trouble with this particular lot is that they were stolen."

"And they are payable to bearer. As a bank with such bonds on offer and at a very advantageous discount, we could not refuse them. And I believe that other banks in Barcelona were influenced in the same way. Indeed, I am told that only this morning a further lot of these bonds was cashed in at no less than twenty per cent, discount. That makes five hundred thousand pounds in all and, you can understand, Mr. Rushton, the good British bonds worth par and to be secured at from fifteen to twenty per cent. discount is a profit which no bank will turn away from in these days."

"I quite see that," admitted Rushton. "Nevertheless, the bonds were stolen."

"But that does not affect banks. They are as good as gold, and the property of bearer. It is for the British Government to catch the thieves or reimburse those who lost them."

"Your point is quite in order. Do you feel disposed to tell me who has cashed them? I understand they were negotiated through a prominent Catalonian politician."

"That is so, or, rather, it would be more correct to say that the person who carried out the transactions was prominent in Catalonian politics. For some time past he has been living very quietly. His name is Count Larida."

Grant Rushton sat up.

"Count Jose Larida?"

"Yes. Do you know him?"

Rushton had never met Larida personally, but he did know that Larida had been hand in glove with "Flash" Brady in the smuggling of arms into the Riff country. And now if it was Larida who was handling the bonds which Brady had stolen, then it all fitted in perfectly with what he and Tony knew so far.

What they did not know was that Larida had handled the bonds against the intention he had originally expressed to Brady. His reason for that will appear presently.

"I know of Larida," was Rushton's non-committal response to the banker's question. "And I have reason to believe I know how it comes that it is he who has negotiated these bonds. Do you know where he lives in Barcelona?"

"He does not reside actually in Barcelona, but some distance away. He left Barcelona and withdrew from participation in politics at the time of his marriage."

"Ah! Can you give me the exact location?"

"Yes. Do you plan, then, to go out there?"

"It is possible."

"I would warn you to move warily, Mr. Rushton. There is a good deal of mystery about Larida and his present household. The place has a sinister atmosphere in rumour."

"Of Larida's own making, perhaps, to his own ends."

"That is possible, but in this case I do not think Larida is responsible. He lives in the *residencia* that belonged to the lady he married. Her family history is a strange one, and among the people of the hills I understand the place is taboo. I have no personal knowledge of the family, but for years and years I remember hearing strange tales about her father— terrible stories were told. I should say that he was probably mad, and terrified the surrounding countryside by his savage deeds."

"As how?"

"You know the sort of thing that is whispered among the ignorant peasants of a country like this when things happen which they do not understand. They say that the old man used to hunt the countryside at night with a pack of enormous black hounds —that, indeed, he was the devil, and that the hounds were phantom hounds. There is no doubt but that there were many strange tragedies among those rugged hills at that time, and a good many people disappeared."

"Somewhat similar to our own Herne the Hunter of Windsor Park," murmured Rushton.

"Yes, but even more sinister. They believed that the old man carried his victims back to his place and, before destroying them, sucked their veins dry."

"A man vampire."

"Exactly."

"How did Larida get tied up with that sort of thing?"

"No one knows. He vanished very suddenly from Barcelona, and the next we heard was that he was living out there, that he had married the old man's daughter, whom few had ever seen."

"Was the old man still alive?"

"No. They say that the night he died a great pillar of fire was seen, and that the old man, sheeted in flame, with his phantom hounds in like state, hunted through the night and vanished, to be seen no more."

"In other words, that he had ridden back to the Pit."

"Exactly."

"Well, I fancy we shall find it difficult to penetrate through such a barrier as that, but, nevertheless, we shall try. We shall not be bound to the hills, but will go and return by air."

"That is an idea; I never thought of that. But move warily, Mr. Rushton, move warily."

Rushton nodded cheerfully. The mysterious bogey tales did not worry him. He knew that the sinister old man who had terrified the ignorant countryside had probably devised the whole thing in order to keep prying people from coming too close. But what reason might lie behind it Rushton could not guess.

When he had received more detailed particulars of the exact situation of the Larida *residencia,* together with more warnings, Rushton returned to the hotel to find Tony. For he had decided that, as it was only a matter of fifty miles or so in each direction, they would make a preliminary scouting flight that same afternoon.

He knew now that Brady had planned the coup with every possible care. Knowing what he did about Larida, it was unthinkable that the master-criminal had simply plumped down upon him without warning.

Larida must have been prepared long ago.

Which meant, according to Rushton's reasoning, that whatever mysteries the *residencia* in the hills might hide, it was open to Brady and friends of that sort.

As a matter of fact, it may be said here that, when he married, Jose Larida had no suspicion of what he had let himself in for.

He had met the woman who was to be his bride during a trip through the mountains when he was secretly trying to stir up the peasants against the Madrid Government.

At that time the sinister old man who had created such gossip was dead—had been dead and gone for some six months.

For once in his life Jose Larida fell head over heel in love. Until that time all women had been nothing to him.

But, as is so often the case, when he did go off the deep end he took a complete plunge.

Gone for the time being was all thought of the aims of the Catalonian party, all schemes of intrigue and subtle crime. He remained in the hills to complete his wooing, and certainly it would have taken a far cleverer man than he to see that behind the smiling mask of her beauty the girl he sought held a tiger of mad jealousy enchained.

If he gave any thought at all, then, to his personal schemes, it was no more than to tell himself that in this lonely *residencia,* far back in the Sierra de Lallena, he had found a perfect fortress to serve as an impregnable retreat. No Spanish soldiers would ever dare to penetrate there, and he had nothing to fear from the Catalonians, with whom he was hand-in-glove. Indeed, it did flash upon him that he would make it his headquarters.

But the rest of his time and thought was given to his wooing, until, when the marriage was over, he found out very soon what a she-devil cat he had taken unto him.

His withdrawal from Catalonian plottings was by no means voluntary, as was believed among his former associates in Barcelona. On the contrary, he would have given all his possessions and risked anything for the escape from his present state to be among them again.

But he was plunged into a vortex of terror that grew as time passed. Away up there in the lonely hills he absorbed the superstitious tales which were current among the peasants, and his fear of this beautiful devil he had married became such an obsession of superstitious dread that he was afraid even to sleep o' nights.

Therefore it can be understood that Brady's first communication came as a rope to a drowning man. It was only by good luck that this reached him without the knowledge of his wife, who at the time was locked in her own apartments in the throes of the strange dementia that seized upon her at every full moon.

Following that, he had arranged with one of the few servants he could trust to receive other letters and post his replies.

It is already known how Brady and Gloria Ravissa were received on their arrival, and how, this time in actual self-defence, the beautiful adventuress shot the countess dead.

The effect upon Count Larida was amazing. Within a few minutes he passed through an extraordinarily swift metamorphosis. The drawn lines on his haggard countenance vanished as if at the touch of a magic hand. His stooped shoulders straightened, and life returned to his lack-lustre eyes. A very different creature stood where the fear-ridden man had been. It was as complete a changing as when the snake sloughs his old skin and appears in brilliant, new, glistening scales.

There was no further talk of using an intermediary in Barcelona. Larida was only too anxious to handle the bonds personally, and it was arranged for him to reach the city early Monday morning.

Little time was spent over the funeral obsequies. The padre was amenable, and all the servants or peasants knew about the affair was that the last of the old line was gone. The gloomy ravines seemed even to grow a little less forbidding with the wiping away of this family that had hovered above them for so many centuries.

As for Brady, things couldn't have gone better. He knew before the shooting that the countess was going to prove difficult. But the whole problem had been solved by Gloria Ravissa as easy as slicing a pat of butter, and now not only did he have Larida as a willing and dependent ally, but he could consider himself in control of the whole *residencia*—a retreat such as was ideal for his purpose until he completed his arrangements to go across to North Africa

But at that moment Brady wasn't so sure that he would cross the Straits of Gibraltar as soon as he had intended. This fortress should provide all his needs, and be inaccessible to anyone on the trail of the bonds.

Thus he told himself on Tuesday and up to a certain hour on Wednesday afternoon.

Then, far in the distance, a flashing speck in the clean blue of the sky over the sierras, appeared something that sent Brady dashing into his room for his binoculars, and, shouting to Gloria and Liddle, up the stairs to the flat roof.

CHAPTER XII   THE RIOT

RUSHTON'S instructions to Tony had been simple.

"You know your objective, Tony. Fly by dead reckoning, and when we spot the place don't go too close until I give the signal. We will see what we can through the glasses."

It was an easy flight from Barcelona. Over the low plains by the sea the Moth skimmed as smoothly as a bird, mounting gradually all the time, while the deep bluey-green of the Mediterranean lengthened behind them and the rugged peaks of the Pyrenees began to show bolder on the northern horizon.

Soon Tony was above the foothills, still climbing, and in that rarer ether, with the cloudless blue above them, they could see down into the glens and valleys as if through a magic glass.

Little streams that would have been invisible from a nearer point stood out like snowy ribbons against the dark background. Tiny dales that scarcely knew the foot of man became revealed as little parks of the gnomes. Paths, secret paths of the hill peasants that no unauthorised person had known for centuries, now lay like pale tan ribbons flung carelessly among masses of greens and browns.

The larger streams were displayed in the complete network which gave them a certain irregular symmetry, if such could be said. Each and all did service to the slopes of the mountains, and burbled along towards the larger river that drained the whole of that part of the water-shed.

Houses were almost non-existent. Here and there could be seen a tiny cluster of huts forming a mountain hamlet, and at rare intervals a small church, dating from many centuries back.

There were, too, the almost invisible hovels of the charcoal-burners and others who lived mysterious and terribly squalid lives among the hills.

But that was all. It was as inaccessible, normally, from Barcelona as if it were a mountain range beyond the Arctic Circle.

It was when they skimmed one sharp, tree-clad ridge that they suddenly picked out their objective.

From over the saddle of the most distant ridge the westering sun was sending its shaft full upon the *residencia.* It was as plain to Rushton and Tony as if it were a house picked out in white upon a black expanse.

The moment they came into view, Rushton lifted his glasses and studied the place, while Tony banked slightly and changed his course to a more westerly point.

But, distant though he was, he knew that they had come right. The *residencia* was as the banker had vaguely described it. But had he needed actual proof, he had it in the sight of the aeroplane that looked little more than a gull, standing with wings outspread on the comparatively broad expanse of the flat roof.

Almost at the same moment Rushton saw a figure burst through on to the roof, followed by two others. Through his glasses he had no difficulty in recognising the three as Brady, Gloria Ravissa, and Liddle.

Rushton signalled quickly to Tony and made a violent movement downwards with his right arm.

The response was so swift that even an experienced aviator might have been excused for feeling the sickening drag that assailed his stomach as Tony banked so swiftly and dived that, within an incredibly brief space of time, they shot earthwards like a bullet, to flatten out only when they were no more than a hundred feet above the trees of a long, narrow ravine, where twilight already laid its shadow and the *residencia* was quite out of sight.

By the time Tony had followed the course of the ravine until he was over the plains the *residencia* was left far, far behind. It was only then that he sought a higher level, and, receiving a further signal from Rushton, laid his course for Barcelona aerodrome.

Rushton said nothing of his intentions until they had run the plane into its hangar and were driving back to the hotel.

"That was the Bat all right, Tony," he said at last, breaking a silence that Tony was thinking would never end.

"It was a 'plane on that roof, but I couldn't see details."

"Well, my glasses showed everything plainly. It was the Bat, and two of three persons who rushed out on to the roof were Brady and Gloria Ravissa.

I don't know whether the third would be Liddle or Larida."

"What's the next step, then?"

"We've got to put that machine out of commission. While they have got it they have a perfect means of getting away whenever they wish. But without it they would be heavily handicapped. It isn't an easy job getting down those mountain paths, although I don't say they couldn't get a car up to the place in some way. We haven't had a chance to study the roads that may have been built privately. But, leaving that for the moment, we must concentrate on that 'plane. A car would mean they were limited in choice. The 'plane gives them freedom to take flight right out of Spain—out of Europe."

"You're dead right there, Chief."

"And Brady saw our 'plane."

"Are you sure?"

"We were undoubtedly spotted in the sky, and that is what brought them rushing on to the roof. He was just raising his glasses when you took that hair-lifting dive."

Tony grinned.

"Sorry if I stirred you up, but I thought you wanted quick action."

"I did—and got it. We were out of sight before Brady could possibly have distinguished anything definite. But if he is suspicious of a 'plane about these mountains, his first thoughts will go to us, for he knew back at Fingest that we were using the Moth."

Tony became more serious.

"By ginger, you're right!"

"And it looks as though they had already succeeded in disposing of most if not all of the bonds."

"Then there isn't anything to stop Brady from making a get-away now."

"None that we know of. Therefore we are going to act as swiftly as possible."

"What will you do?"

"We have two choices as far as I can see, neither of which is going to recover the bonds, but each of which might put us in a way to get possession of the money Brady has received for them."

"Which are the choices?"

"Well, firstly, we could fly to the place and chance a landing on the roof. It is an excellent idea to use that as a landing-ground, and I dare say that if we had been closer, we would have seen that the parapet at one end has been cleared away, so that a machine can take off."

"The pilot would do a nice somersault if it wasn't!"

"Exactly! We will say that you could succeed in bringing the Moth down beside the Bat—"

"Of course I could!" interrupted Tony vigorously. "I can put the

102

Moth wherever that bird Liddle can place the Bat, and in a smaller one, too!"

"All right! All right!" snapped Rushton testily. "I wasn't impugning your ability as a pilot. Let me proceed!"

"Sorry, chief."

"From our experience to-day it is plain that we would not be permitted to get far without meeting with opposition. We have no means of knowing how much of a force Larida has in that place. It is large enough to accommodate a goodly number with ease—two score, at any rate. If we failed to overcome such possible and probable resistance, we should find ourselves in a nice mess, and you know about what short shrift we'd get from Brady in a lonely place like that."

"I know that all right."

"Our second or alternative hope would be to fly to the place and destroy the Bat without landing. If we could do that we should have succeeded in cutting off Brady's most important means of making a getaway."

"How do you mean?"

"If we could get hold of a bomb of only mildly explosive force it would do the trick. We don't know who is in the house besides the crooks. I shouldn't like to cause injury to innocent persons. But that is a substantial-looking roof, and I believe a bomb of the right force accurately dropped would put the Bat out of commission without doing much serious damage to the roof."

Tony's eyes danced.

"By ginger, that's the wheeze, chief! How can we get that bomb? I can bring the Moth down almost on top of the Bat, so all you would have to do would be to toss the bomb into her."

"It's not quite as easy as that, particularly if Brady and the others are popping at us with rifles or pistols. There is no guessing what sort of arsenal Larida keeps there. But there are a good many places where one can find bombs in Barcelona. They are always pitching them into something round about here. It's an old Spanish custom. I know a man who might put me on the track of what we want, but it is too late to think of returning to the *residencia* this evening. It will be dusk in another half-hour. To-night we will see what we can find."

They had been talking in the lounge of the hotel where they were staying. Ordinarily Rushton would have gone to one of the big modern hotels in the new part of the city, where among those wide boulevards with their exact lines of plane trees one might have thought oneself in Paris or Madrid, or even Berlin. Such was new Barcelona.

But Rushton had chosen to go to a smaller, much quieter though very comfortable hotel in the old city, where the streets are as narrow and winding as in the old parts of Paris or Marseilles, and where all the whispered plottings of the Catalans have their birth.

He was not anxious to run into any English or other foreigners whom he might know. He knew that it was quite possible that Brady would have contacts with the foreign element, and did he mix in it, precious little time would be lost before his movements were reported to Brady.

Not that he minded now if Brady were told of his presence. He knew that Brady knew that he was there. On the other hand, he did not want his every movement reported.

From where they sat they could see through the windows of the lounge right out on to the Rambla, that fine old thoroughfare that winds up across the old city and stands very favourable comparison with the more ornate streets of the new quarter.

It, too, is lined with plane trees, and from under these Rushton saw Senor Rimera, the banker, walking quickly from where he had left a taxi at the kerb.

The moment he entered the lounge he spotted Rushton and came across.

"I was hoping to catch you in, Mr. Rushton," were his words as he dropped down beside them. "I have some news for you. It has just come to me through a man whose identity I must keep undisclosed."

"Certainly, Senor Rimera. What is your news?"

"The Countess Larida is dead—very suddenly."

"Dead! Good heavens! Do you think this has any bearing on Larida's recent activities?"

"I don't know. I can't even guess. I am going to tell you all I know, which is little enough."

"You are good to take this trouble."

"I wish to help you if I can. I am worried about these bonds. This is what I have been told. The Countess Larida has been dead for about three days. No one knows just what happened at the *residencia*, but it is known definitely that the local padre was called in, and that a certificate of death and burial had been secured. It is believed that the funeral will take place either to-night or tomorrow, the interment to be in the ground attached to a private chapel on the estate."

Both Rushton and Tony remembered having seen a small building like a chapel, a little distance from the mansion, but within the surrounding boundaries of the place.

"As I say, nothing definite is known; but whispers have gone abroad, and it is already said by the peasants that she died by violence. This does not mean that they hold anything against Larida. On the contrary. My information goes to show that they say Larida is a changed man, and, indeed, from other sources I find that he was very different in manner when he was in Barcelona these last few days than he had ever been before. The peasants are glad enough that the last of that family is gone. No one will ever know more than Larida chooses to allow to come out of the place. But I thought you ought to know this, in case it might have some bearing on your business."

"If it has caused a metamorphosis in Larida it well might," said Rushton slowly. "You do not know if Larida is still in Barcelona?"

"I cannot tell you."

"If I could only intercept him," muttered Rushton. "He may have been here to-day. And it may even be that he is returning to-night for the funeral, if your information is correct. I am most awfully obliged for all the trouble you have taken, Senor Rimera. It may be that I shall be able to use the information."

"I hope so."

The banker excused himself from refreshment, as he lived some distance out in the suburb of Horta, and was already late in getting home.

Rushton and Tony dined quietly. It was Rushton's intention that they should get into native clothes and go more deeply into the old city in search of the person who, he knew, would be willing enough to help him. Rushton had a good many such contacts in many strange places all over the world, for he knew from experience that such contacts with the criminal underworld were at times far more valuable in running his man down than any amount of police assistance or personal effort.

But Fate was destined to take a hand before they could put their plan into effect.

Even before dinner there seemed, to both Rushton and Tony, an air of something like suppressed excitement or nervousness about the hotel.

It had not been marked enough to cause them to give it any particular attention. Yet it had been there, and with the departure of the banker Rushton had more attention to give to his immediate surroundings.

The hotel, as has been said, was on the Rambla, the ancient main thoroughfare of the old city. It was a hostelry to which scarcely any foreigners, Americans or British, ever penetrated.

On the other hand, it was very popular among the Catalans from outside Barcelona and among Spaniards from all over Spain. It ranked, indeed, among the people of the country just about as one of the solid old county hotels would rank in England.

It was fairly well patronised at the present time, for this was the period of the year when many of the conservative country folk came in to do their semi-annual shopping.

Until this evening Rushton and Tony had had little opportunity to observe their fellow-guests, and few curious glances were thrown their way, for, as usual, they were dressed quietly, and, like seasoned travellers, conducted themselves according to the customs of the country.

Nevertheless, it was impossible to miss a certain constrained air that seemed to hang about waiters and guests alike in the gloomy old dining-room.

There seemed to be much whispering, much low-toned conversation, and, unusual among those people, a great deal of rustling of evening newspapers at the table.

Rushton and Tony had been so engaged with their own affairs that they had not even glanced at a local paper since their arrival. But now, as they pursued their meal and noticed that something in the sheets seemed to be the cause of subdued apprehension, Rushton sent a waiter for some copies, and the moment they opened them out they had the clue.

Each sheet displayed in large letters some political slogan, and, reading, it soon became evident that the revolutionistic Catalan party was once more at loggerheads with the Central Government in Madrid, while, on the other hand, the internal Catalan parties were again at daggers drawn.

Rushton held no brief for any side in Catalan politics. It was all the same to him whatever party might be in power. But he had to regard the present situation as it might affect his own interests.

There had been no hint in the English Press before they left London that another blow-up in Barcelona was imminent. But that meant nothing. The pot was always simmering in Barcelona, and the lid might go off at any moment, as he knew.

Here, however, in these evening journals was disturbing news. Clashes in the main city were, it was affirmed, imminent. Disturbances seemed to be threatening in a dozen different quarters of the city, and every party, no matter what its aims, appeared to be out on the rampage.

"We seem to have arrived at an interesting time, old son," remarked Rushton in a low tone.

"I haven't seen any signs of trouble. Have you?"

"No; but that doesn't mean anything here. At the same time this newspaper stuff may be all fizz. Yet our neighbours and the hotel staff don't seem any too cheerful. I felt that something was hanging over the place, and yet I could not place it. But this is it."

He saw that the waiter was trying to listen to their conversation, so he changed it. He did not question the man on the subject, for there was no knowing what party he might belong to, and little information would be gained.

The first definite hint that the newspaper stuff was not all "fizz," as Rushton had said, came just as they were leaving the dining-room to pass into the lounge.

From somewhere in the lower (modern) city there came the sound of a deep, muffled explosion.

Like magic everyone who was in the lounge, seated, standing or in movement, froze into a rigid position of listening, as if a spell had been laid upon him or her.

Boom!

A second deep roar, less muffled, came up the Rambla, the concussion being sufficient to jar the main doors inwards and outwards.

Boom!

A third explosion was even nearer, and, seemingly, more violent. And this served to snap the frozen listeners into action.

Some of the women uttered low cries of fright, and immediately sought their men-folk. Men looked furtively about them, and sought deep corners, or else, as in the case of Rushton and Tony, rushed to the front doors to get into the street to see what there was.

Out there fresh sound greeted their ears, although on the Rambla itself there was no sign of anything untoward.

These fresh sounds were the sharp racketings of pistols, rifles or machine-guns—it was impossible to tell at the distance. Then followed another great boom, and, down somewhere in the new city, they could see a great pillar of flame arise.

"They're attacking the trams," Rushton and Tony heard one old country gentleman assert. "It was threatened."

"Do you think it is serious?" asked Rushton courteously.

The old gentleman looked at him for a moment.

"Inglesa, senor?"

"Yes, sir, English."

"Then you had best keep clear of it. It may be only much noise with little wounding, as sometimes happens, or it may be the nasty affair that is always being promised. If it is confined to the lower city it may blow over. But if the people from the old quarter beyond us take a hand it may develop into a real clash."

They listened once more.

The heavy sounds, Rushton concluded, were made by the explosion of bombs, and now, for a little while, they heard no more of these. On the other hand, there was rising above the rattle of the guns that dreadful sound than which there is nothing more sinister or more menacing—the roar of an angry mob.

It seemed to mount as the flames spread and lifted into the sky. It punctuated each volley of the shooting, and there was in it, Rushton and Tony could hear, that element which drives every mob to extremes—women.

From their vantage-point on the Rambla they could also see the myriad lights of the great city, where the boulevards lay at regular form, and along most of the vast harbour front, where shipping from all the world lay.

Suddenly one boulevard seemed to vanish entirely. Every light had winked out in the space of a moment, and while they watched, another and another bevy of lights plunged into darkness.

"Some of the bombs, at any rate, have done some damage," Tony heard Rushton mutter. "But—"

He got no further. In one swoop every light along the Rambla went out, leaving them blinking in a sudden darkness that was all the more accentuated from the previous glow.

While they stood, staring a little stupidly, the racket in the lower town became more and more confusing. Now there were boomings which could only come from artillery, which meant that, whoever the rioters might be, the State troops and police were in action.

Their attention, however, was soon caught by a new noise. This seemed to come from higher up in the old town, behind where they stood.

It was more like a distant but growing echo of the racket in the lower town than anything else.

First it began with a low, humming sound that was scarcely perceptible above the other medley. But it grew steadily in volume and pitch until it became definitely established as of its own. And then it leaped into a terrifying outbreak of confusion all of a sudden.

The Spaniard standing beside Rushton paled, and, muttering something about the saints, trotted back into the hotel. Rushton saw others follow him, and then a woman screamed.

"The *moufs* are out!"

The *moufs,* both Rushton and Tony knew, referred to the worst criminal classes, who were a festering sore in that part of the old town.

Their politics were negligible, unless one could say that they were always against authority of every sort.

Like rats, they lurked in their warren, watching their chance to burst forth and scavenge whenever chance offered. And they evidently thought that this night offered such a chance.

Furthermore, Rushton knew that of late years there had been a terrific influx of desperate characters to that part, and that they had achieved a crude sort of political creed with which they cloaked their many crimes. They were the sort of rabble picked up by people like Larida and used for any immediate purpose, their reward being what they could gain by general looting in the confusion. And thus, under a political cloak, they went scot-free, as did the legitimate Catalans.

The woman was a resident of the quarter. As soon as she had uttered the words she turned and fled into a narrow side-street.

Looking in either direction, Rushton could see that everyone near at hand on the Rambla was likewise rushing for shelter.

He could see no signs of the rioters yet, but the noise at the steep end of the Rambla was rising to a greater and greater din each moment, and he knew that very soon the mob must debouch on to the boulevard.

He had almost forgotten the rioting in the lower city, but now, as he turned in that direction, he saw another great pillar of flame, wreathed in black smoke, shoot into the sky, and a terrific explosion followed.

It was plain that Barcelona was in for a bad night.

He felt Tony touch his arm.

"What will we do, guv'nor? Are you going to stick by the hotel, or make a break into the city?"

"We'll stick here for the present, my lad. I wish we were well out of this and on our way to the aerodrome. There's no chance to start now, but if we find an opportunity we'll make a break for there. Thank goodness, most of our belongings that matter are out there. But this puts the lid on our getting a bomb for the purpose I had in mind."

"That gang has them all," returned Tony, as a sudden explosion took place far up the Rambla, and then, in the succeeding light, they saw the mob, packed tightly, as, yelling and cheering hoarsely, it swept down upon them.

CHAPTER XIII   A NIGHT OF TERROR

RUSHTON and Tony made for the hotel. They were just in time before a panic-stricken waiter barred the doors upon them. Then every light in the place went out.

Women began to scream hysterically in the darkness, and men began to shout for lights. The sounds of shooting, yelling, and bombing up the street grew more and more portentous. It seemed to Rushton as though the rioters were hurling bombs and blazing away with firearms quite indiscriminately.

He thought, too, he could make out the occasional shattering of glass, which meant, he supposed, that the mob was breaking and looting as it came.

Quite aside from the guests in the lounge, the waiters and rest of the staff were in dire confusion.

One, it is true, had found a candle, and had lit it. But this served only to accentuate the fear that held everyone. And, to make matters worse, those who had been upstairs were now finding their way down, loudly asking questions or panicking hysterically.

Another and another candle was lit, and, with the composed voice of the manager, a little of the terror began to subside. But no more had it done so than there came a terrific explosion outside in the street, and the very building rocked as some of the glass in windows and doors came hurtling inwards.

The screams now rose to a pitch of uncontrolled fear. The yelling mob rushed into the lounge after the wreckage, and then came a terrific battering at the door as the rats strove to break the barrier.

It was as if they had suddenly realised that here was rich plucking, and were determined to get at it.

Rushton and Tony had stood in one corner up to now. But with the inrush of the rioters they hesitated no longer.

"Shoot, young 'un," Rushton snapped. "Let 'em have it! I'm not going to stand here and let them run over us without putting up a fight!"

Their weapons roared almost on the same instant. Then someone else shot on the other side of the lounge, and a momentary check of movement and voice seemed to seize upon the mob.

But it broke with fresh yells almost at once, and right into the crowd of terrified guests and waiters came hurtling another bomb.

Had that bomb been of a really powerful nature, it would have created awful massacre among those closely packed people. As it was, it served sufficiently to wreck more of the lounge, to break through the front doors, and to sweep several persons within the range of its explosion.

It was no more than a home-made affair, however, as Rushton's trained ear realised, and telling himself that the gang could not have many more such weapons, he pushed forward, and, with Tony beside him, made a stand by the door.

Their shooting was deadly. The bullets poured right into the legs of the mass that was trying to press forward, and, realising that here was defence such as they had not looked for, the front ranks tried to draw back, while those behind kept pushing them forward.

The pandemonium inside the lounge was indescribable. That outside was like the ravening of wild beasts.

Rushton stopped shooting when he knew he had only a couple of cartridges left in his clip, and, bending down, told Tony to empty his and refill.

He did so, and, as soon as he was shooting again, Rushton refitted a fresh clip and started again.

Against this determined and punishing resistance the mob could not make headway. Now, those behind knew that something was wrong in front, but they could not make out just what it was.

In front of Rushton and Tony were a dozen or more of the gang piled wounded on top of each other, forming a barricade over which those who pressed could not pass.

And all the time that deadly hail of lead kept raining into their limbs.

Rushton and Tony were scarcely aware that the other man with the gun had joined them, and was also shooting. They only realised it when, with a yell, he leaped against the crushing mass, and, after emptying his weapon, drew a knife, which he began to thrust in any and every direction.

Then, in the midst of the turmoil, Rushton became aware that one of the rioters had climbed over the barrier of bodies, and was leaping straight towards him, his hand upraised.

From somewhere a fugitive gleam of light showed him the object in the fellow's hand was neither knife nor pistol, but an irregularly shaped thing that looked not unlike a tin canister.

In a flash he knew it for a bomb, which it was plain the other intended to hurl straight into his face.

There was no chance to retreat; there was no gain in dodging. The only possible way to tackle the sudden threat of horrible death was to stop the deed entirely. And Rushton went to it.

He leapt straight at the fellow, meeting him upon the yielding mass of the wounded. His left hand thrust out hard and caught the other's wrist in its forward sweep, and then, while the home-made bomb left the clutching fingers and began to carry on towards Rushton, he thrust the wrist away and snapped up his hand to catch the bomb.

For one tense moment as his fingers curled round it and he held it—a battered old tin canister of sorts—he expected the thing to explode and rip him to pieces.

He knew a good deal about such bombs, and knew that it all depended on what sort it might be— a time bomb, a fuse bomb, or one that depended for its explosion upon violent contact.

If it were the first or the second, then he hadn't a hope if the mechanism was in working order. But, if it were the third, and his checking of its flight had not been too violent, then it might have no more effect than a dud.

Tony had seen what was happening, and, jumping in, drove off Rushton's assailant, shooting at point-blank range as he did so. From behind them fresh firing started, showing that some of the men among the guests had pulled themselves together and got their weapons.

It was this or, possibly, a fresh outburst in the lower town, that caused the rioters to sway back, and then, as suddenly and as wantonly as they had begun the attack, they left it and swept on down the Rambla, leaving the dead and wounded to care for themselves as best they might.

Rushton was still holding the bomb gingerly, but, as the mob passed on, he turned to Tony.

"Guide me through the lounge some way. Be careful I don't smash into anything. I want to get up to our rooms quickly."

Under cover of the confusion, Tony got hold of his arm and guided him through the smoky, candlelit lounge. It was already known that it was due to the prompt stand made by Rushton and Tony that the mob had been held off, and many men would have intercepted them.

But the lad managed to elbow a way through and get Rushton on to the staircase. They still had to run the gauntlet of other terrified guests still descending, but eventually they reached their rooms, where Rushton very gingerly laid the bomb on the table.

Even in the gloom and smoky confusion below he had seen that the bomb was only of crude manufacture. Now, at close candlelight, it was even more obvious that the thing had been manufactured from a large tin canister.

A close study convinced Rushton that it was a "contact" bomb, that is, one that depended for its explosion upon a violent blow to bring contact inside between some form of striker and the discharging cap.

They had both noticed that the bombs that had been exploded against the front of the hotel and in the lounge had burst immediately upon contact with the ground, so it seemed safe to assume that this one was of a similar nature, and simply one of the store of crude weapons which the rats in the deeper part of the quarter manufactured in their spare time against just some such need as this night.

When he was satisfied that it contained neither a timing fuse nor a clockwork control, Rushton lifted his head.

"This might just about do the job."

Tony had already grasped what he intended.

"You mean—to bomb the Bat?"

"Yes. We were going out to try to get hold of such a contrivance, or the materials for making one, but it has come right into our hands instead."

"Into your hands, you mean."

"Never mind how it came, so long as we have it. The next thing is, though, to reach the aerodrome. It will be impossible to go by the usual way to-night. Heaven knows when they will settle down now. This upheaval may last for days."

"All the better for our stunt," returned Tony optimistically.

"And all the better for Brady's stunt. His stars are working for him, Tony. Everything fell just the way he wanted it back in England; and he has managed to dispose of those bonds here in Barcelona just before this outbreak. It couldn't have been arranged better for him. It may be days before the Barcelona banks are open again for the transaction of ordinary business; and all this confusion will form a perfect cloak for Brady and his gang to make a getaway."

"Unless we stop him."

"Exactly—unless we stop him."

"Where do you think he will make for?"

"Almost undoubtedly the Riff country in Morocco. But we've got to stop him, my lad. Once he gets into the Riff country with that bunch of money we'll never see it again—never. You can fly to-night?"

"Of course," snorted Tony. "Blind flying is my stunt. Besides, we'll have a moon later. It won't be as good as the one we had at Fingest, but it will be above the horizon about midnight."

"And in this clear atmosphere will be even better," supplemented Rushton. "Well, come on, then, let's stuff our pockets with what small stuff we need and can carry. We need to get going. The rest of our luggage will have to remain here until we can pick it up again."

They set to work, and in a few minutes were ready to start. Rushton had taken pains to pack the bomb carefully in a small attache-case and carry it under his left arm so as to avoid direct contact with anyone.

It was easy enough to get through the lounge and out into the Rambla. The excitable Latins were still jabbering away when they descended, and, so far, no one seemed to have succeeded in producing any more light than that given by a dozen or so candles.

The bodies of the dead and wounded were still in the street, and as they crossed the Rambla, Rushton and Tony could see no signs of any police or troops.

Down the lower city the racket still continued, though on a somewhat more subdued scale. But that meant nothing. A fresh outburst might come at any moment. As a matter of fact, the mob at that moment was busy overturning tram-cars, and for the next three days Barcelona was in a state of upheaval.

When they were across the Rambla and had dived into a narrower street that ran at right angles, Tony turned inquiringly to Rushton.

"How are we going?"

"I've got an idea, Tony. If we cut right across the old town and descend the hill on the western side, we'll come to Horta. It is a comparatively short journey compared to the way in which Senor Rimera would go in his car. If we can knock him up we shall borrow his car to go out to the 'drome."

"That's a brain-wave."

"We've got to get there first," grunted Rushton.

But it was not difficult. Most of the criminal classes lived in the warren higher up beyond the Rambla, and here the district through which they were passing was occupied mostly by small tradespeople and civil servants, who were only too glad to remain behind locked doors and shutters while the mob raised a rumpus in the city.

They even passed an occasional policeman, but they said nothing, nor were they accosted, the patrols not being anxious to be brought into any closer contact with the disturbance that hung over Barcelona that night.

Their way took them right over the flank of the hill formed by the old city, and, once they began to descend the steep streets on the other side, they heard and saw nothing more of the rioting.

Here were more solidly-built houses, which became even better as they went down into the suburb of Horta. And in Horta they found the very substantial residences of well-off business men, bankers, and professional men.

They found, too, a greater frequency of policemen, and through one of these they were directed to the *residencia* of Senor Rimera.

The banker was not in bed. Like a good many other law-abiding citizens of Barcelona, he was sitting up while the mob in the city played havoc, and when they were ushered into his study, they found him on the telephone to the watchman of his bank.

He was, of course, surprised to see the two Englishmen, but when he heard what Rushton wanted, he consented readily.

"As a matter of fact, I will drive out with you," he said. "I was debating whether I should risk going into the city. I don't think the mob can get at the bank, but I am somewhat worried. What can you tell me about the trouble, Mr. Rushton? I didn't hear a whisper of this before I left the city. It must have broken very suddenly."

"It did. The gang from the old city are out as well. They have wrecked a good deal of the Rambla."

Rushton told him as much as he and Tony had seen and experienced of the rioting. Rimera shook his head.

"It's always been the same through the history of Barcelona," he said moodily, "and it has been particularly bad since the War. For some days the city will be littered with debris, and then things will go on as usual. But one of these days the mob will really get the upper hand, and then—pouf!"

The aerodrome gave no signs that anything was amiss in the city. An air-liner had just left for Paris and London, and the landing-ground was brilliantly lighted in anticipation of the arrival of two night mail-'planes, one from Paris and one from Rome.

The Moth was in a small hangar at the far end of the ground, and after seeing Senor Rimera drive away, Rushton and Tony went along to attend to some slight formalities and to get the latest dope on flying conditions.

Then they entered the hangar, to find one of the 'drome mechanics still at work going over the Moth. Tony dismissed him, and then he and Rushton sat down on a box in one corner to wait for the first sign of the moon.

While they sat there they heard a certain amount of activity outside, but paid it no attention, for each was engrossed in his own thoughts.

From time to time Tony peered to the east for sight of the first glow of the rising moon, and the moment he saw the tell-tale paling he touched Rushton on the arm.

As Tony had said, he had done a good deal of blind flying, and now the journey to the Larida *residencia* was not difficult, although he took the precaution of flying much higher than by day, for the jutting ridges of the sierras were very deceptive in the shadow.

But the waning moon was shining full on the eastern flank of the mountains when they reached their objective, and this, white-washed and detached, stood out weirdly distinct in the moonlight.

Nevertheless, it needed every care for the lad to bring the Moth round and bank so as to get into position for the swoop across the roof of the house.

On the way from the landing-ground Rushton had opened the attache-case, and was all ready to drop the bomb as soon as Tony got his position.

Thus they were as the Moth dived steeply, and then, flattening out, zoomed straight across the long flat roof of the *residencia* from end to end, and not more than fifty feet above it.

It was a perfect position for Rushton's effort. A dozen efforts couldn't have achieved more.

And, bracing himself easily, Rushton held his crude bomb ready to let go at the correct moment.

But even as his fingers prepared to loosen, and while he stared down trying to pick out his target with certainty, he saw the bomb would only be wasted.

The other aeroplane was not to be seen.

CHAPTER XIV   THE ATTACK

TONY lifted one hand, and Rushton knew he had also seen the empty roof.

He withdrew the bomb and signalled for his assistant to carry on. He glanced down again as the 'plane began to mount once more, but the roof showed no signs of any living being, just a blank, moon-washed surface.

Rushton put on the earphones and spoke.

"Back to the aerodrome," was his order.

Not until they were in the hangar did he speak again. Then he sat down on the same upturned box they had occupied before and lit his pipe.

"So that's a wash-out," he grunted.

"What on earth do you suppose has become of it, chief? If that blighter has got away, I'll never forgive myself. It was a peach of a chance to smash that Bat."

"We don't know where he's gone, but he's gone. It is up to us to figure what has become of him. But it looks as if he'd made a pretty good attempt at a getaway."

"I'll say it does."

"Just the same, if Larida sticks to him he can't do it in one flight."

"How do you mean?"

"Well, the Bat won't carry more than three, and, with Larida, they are four."

"I'd forgotten that. There's Brady, Gloria Ravissa, Larida and Liddle, unless they drop Liddle, and I don't believe Brady would do that while he needs the Bat."

"I agree. Therefore it means that they've got to make at least two journeys to get away from that place in the mountains. Moreover, there is the problem of fuel. We know that Brady probably made a direct flight from Fingest to Larida's place. That isn't by any means the full cruising distance of the Bat, but I don't believe he would risk continuing for any great mileage without refilling."

"He'd be crazy if he did."

"Well, then, our first problem is to decide on where he is going to refuel. The normal place would be, of course, right here on this 'drome, but Brady will avoid Barcelona like the plague—if he can.

What other places are there near here? He wouldn't go as far as Madrid. He and Larida will shun everything in Spain."

"He could fill up at Sitjes," muttered Tony.

Rushton nodded.

"He could. That's worth considering. Let's see, Sitjes is right along the coast, some twenty odd miles, isn't it."

"And right on the shore. It's easy enough to land there, but one couldn't do it by moonlight—too many sand dunes."

"But he'd have to make arrangements about having petrol and oil brought, and that would make them conspicuous. And supposing I am right in thinking that Brady will try to make the Riff country in Morocco the one place in the world where he would be absolutely safe from pursuit, then it means the Bat would have to cover between seven and eight hundred miles from here in flying down the east coast of Spain and crossing the Straits of Gibraltar. That knocks off a pretty good lump of her full cruising mileage, my lad."

"She can do eighteen hundred at a pinch, as I told you at Fingest."

"All right. Then that means she would be stretching out pretty well to half her limit. Then if there were difficulty in getting a refill in the Riff, she would not do much more than get back here on the complete filling."

"Just about do it with a bit to spare."

"If Brady follows this line, then how is he going to transport his party—that is, how will he divide them? Will he have Liddle take him and Gloria Ravissa first, or will he send Larida and the girl—or Larida alone? But whichever plan he adopts, we can be dead sure of one thing—Brady will keep the money close in his own care."

"I'll say he will. I'll tell you what I think I'd better do, chief."

"Go on."

"Do a little snooping around the aerodrome and see if there are any signs of the Bat."

"A good idea, but go warily. We don't know exactly where Larida stands around here. I'm beginning to suspect that uprising in Barcelona tonight wasn't all due to spontaneous combustion."

Tony slid out from under the temporary canvas curtain they had dropped—the hangar was only an erection of wooden framing and canvas walls and roof—and mooched off through the shadows at one side of the landing-ground.

A big 'plane came in just as he started, and while almost everyone who was up and about was running across the ground to meet it, Tony had a good chance to inspect several of the other hangars.

In none of them, however, did he see any signs of the Bat, but when he ran into a mechanic who had done a job for him earlier, he pulled him up and made to pay him for his trouble.

In the transaction he held up a fifty-peseta note which he added to the rest.

"I want some information, *hombre,* if you can give it to me."

The man looked at Tony slyly in the gloom. These *Inglesas* were funny people, but they always paid well.

"What do you want to know, senor?" he rejoined softly.

"I'm wanting information about a 'plane that may have been on the landing-ground to-night."

He described the Bat minutely.

The man began to wag his head in the Spanish sign of assent before Tony had finished.

"Why, yes, senor," he said in the same soft tones, "I have seen such a machine. It was on the ground here less than two hours ago."

"It refuelled?"

"*Si,* senor, it took the tanks full of essence and oil."

"Did you see how many persons were in it?"

"Three, I think, senor, but I could not be sure. Give me a moment to think."

Tony flashed another fifty peseta note.

"Perhaps this will help you," he suggested.

The fellow grinned and took the bribe.

"There were three persons, that is right, senor. There was, I think, a senora, but I could not see distinctly, as she did not show her features."

"Who else?"

"The pilot, senor, and another senor. He had, I think, a beard."

"Brady," muttered the lad inaudibly.

"Do you know whither they were bound?"

"No, senor. They did not disclose. They simply refuelled, complied with the formalities of the ground, and took the air again."

"I'm much obliged to you."

"Many thanks, senor."

Tony hot-footed it back to Rushton, who still sat smoking on the upturned box.

"They risked landing here, chief," he said excitedly in low tones. "They refuelled with petrol and oil and went off at once. And, from what I can gather, it looks as if Brady, Gloria Ravissa, and Liddle were in the machine so Larida must have been left behind."

Grant Rushton was about to reply, but before he could do so there came the sharp crack of a pistol just outside the canvas close to which they sat, and both Tony and Rushton dived to the ground as a bullet, ripped through the canvas, ripped past Rushton's ear and went on out through the opposite wall.

Considering the fact that the pistol had obviously been fired only a short distance away from the hangar and that the light of the lantern inside cast Rushton's shadow large and distinct against the canvas, it is amazing that the bullet did not plunge into his skull.

Had the would-be assassin aimed at his body, a miss would have been impossible. But Rushton had been saved, as a matter of fact, by the fact that the shadow of his head on the wall was considerably enlarged.

Once they were on the ground they did not remain there. They both knew perfectly well that the shot was no accidental discharge, but a deliberate attempt at murder.

Nor did they think there had been any mistake in identity. Both were guessing that if it had been Brady, Gloria Ravissa and Liddle who had departed in the Bat, then the would-be assassin must be Larida or someone acting directly under his or Brady's orders.

If that were so, then it meant that Brady was quite aware that there was a good chance of picking them off at the 'drome, and was determined that this be done without delay. In other words, to stop them at Barcelona once and for all.

The two dived out under the canvas hanging over the front and, jerking out their automatics as they ran, flung round the corner of the hangar.

Here, as soon as one got away from the formal layout of the 'drome, one came immediately upon the dense, almost tropical profusion of vegetation which stretches all along the plains on which Barcelona is situated between the two rivers, Besos and Llobregat.

As they appeared another shot burst just ahead of them in the dense undergrowth, and this second noise must have attracted some attention on the landing-ground, for out of the corner of his eye Tony saw two men start and run their way.

But the roar of a big 'plane soon drowned the sound of everything else, and as Rushton and Tony burst into the tangle, shooting at the spot where they had seen the flash, the two men stopped and turned back, thinking it had only been the sound of another engine after all.

Rushton and Tony saw none of that. They knew that they were definitely close to the person who had tried to murder Rushton, and they were determined to get him.

They soon discovered that their quarry was as desperate as he was daring. They had entered the tangle less than ten feet when a third shot flashed on their left and a bullet kicked through the leaves and into the soft soil between them.

They fired again at the flash, and then with one accord dived to the right.

They could hear sounds of crashing beyond for a few moments, then everything became still. Not even from the 'drome did any sound come for this brief space.

It was with the renewed roar of an engine that fresh shots came from the unknown, and then, throwing aside all attempt at keeping cover, Rushton leaped up.

"Come on! I'm going after that beggar!" he shouted to Tony.

A rapid volley of shots split the gloom ahead as Rushton went crashing through the vegetation, but, reckless now, he did not check but followed by Tony, kept straight on.

Suddenly he stumbled out on to a narrow path. Someone was waiting there, for a terrific explosion burst just on his left, and a bullet caught the peak of his cap, jerking it round sideways.

Rushton flung his arm round and fired. Then he saw Tony's weapon flash, and as he made a dive along the path heard Tony yelling:

"I've got him! I've got him! Quick!"

Rushton literally low-tackled into the darkness towards where Tony's voice had sounded. He couldn't have told whether he would grasp branches or something human.

The moment his fingers came into contact he knew that it was human. He grabbed at the first thing and found it to be a leg. He hung on and worked his way along while the body beneath him twisted and contorted like that of an acrobat.

Then he felt Tony's limbs as he twisted over his capture who, in his turn, was struggling like a wildcat and cursing in Spanish worse than any old villain of a pirate who had ever sailed the Spanish Main.

Between them they subdued the fellow, and when they had got his gun and Rushton had twisted him on to his face with one arm jammed up between his shoulder-blades, Tony returned to the hangar to get some cord and a flash-light from the cockpit of the Moth.

When he returned and put the flash on to their prisoner they saw the features of one who, "Flash" Brady could have told them, was Count Jose Larida.

But they didn't need Brady to tell them that after Rushton had taken a look at some of the papers in the other's inside pocket. They knew then all right that it was Larida.

And as they lugged him back cautiously to the hangar, Rushton was again giving some thought to the strange coincidence of the sudden outbreak in Barcelona that night, and the—to Brady—very convenient joining in of the rats from the criminal quarter.

Once they were close to the hangar they laid their burden down and peered across the landing-ground.

The big 'plane that had come in a few minutes before was still claiming the attention of all those who were about, so it was no difficult matter for Rushton and Tony to slither round the corner and in under the canvas flap.

Then with one accord they dumped the burden in the cockpit of the Moth.

"It's Larida all right, and I'm not sure that I like our catch."

"Why not? The blighter tried to murder you."

"A miss is as good as a mile," responded Rushton philosophically. "The reason I don't like it is this: I don't believe that uprising in Barcelona to-night is mere coincidence with Brady's getaway. We know from what Senor Rimera said that Larida has been mixed up to the neck in Catalan politics and plottings."

"He's a good plotter all right, and he doesn't mind whom he shoots."

"Well, I know that he is, or was, a big influence among the worst classes. It wouldn't take much for him to start going a show such as broke out to-night. It could appear a lot on the surface with nothing very much underneath. But the rumpus would be enough to tie up

Barcelona thoroughly and to keep the police and State troops altogether too busy to waste any time over a crook like Brady, whose crime, after all, was perpetrated in England."

"Hum! You're saying something there."

"You see, young 'un, there was no crime in cashing in those bonds here. They were stolen, of course, but the banks couldn't refuse the money if they chose to make the transactions; and, believe me, in these times not many banks are going to let pass a chance to get the best class of British Government bearer bonds at fifteen and twenty per cent discount."

"You mean they couldn't touch Brady on that?"

"Not on the actual transaction. If we had made formal charges against him or, better still, Mark Errol had allowed Scotland Yard to take official notice, then, application could have been made here for Brady's arrest and detention until the necessary papers should be brought out from England by an officer from the Yard. Brady may have figured that something like that was being done. At any rate, it is my guess that through Larida he staged this whole show to-night just so as to cover his getaway and effectually blanket all pursuit. Then, of course, he knew we were here, and he charged Larida to get on our track and finish us off. Larida knew we must come to the 'drome at some time or other. It wasn't difficult. And you could bump off a score of persons round about this part to-night without much inquiry being made."

"If you are right, then Brady didn't forget much."

"I'm thinking he didn't," agreed Rushton savagely. "It means, Tony, that Brady played the winning trick in the first rubber back in England; that he has played a winning trick in the second rubber here in Spain. But there's got to be a third rubber to this set."

"What can we do then?"

"We can't go back into the city—not with Larida. We shouldn't last any longer than a puff of smoke. And we can't hang about here indefinitely."

Tony rubbed his chin thoughtfully while Rushton walked to the door and looked out. When he returned he was gazing at the Moth.

"When I bought that machine for you, Tony," he said slowly, "I told you to get the latest and fastest thing they could turn you out in this class."

"Why, yes," agreed Tony wonderingly. "And I'll say they did a peach of a job. She's all there, as you know yourself from the flight out."

"I know. But she is built to carry only two persons. To-night she's got to carry three."

Tony came to his feet with a grin.

"Don't you worry about that. She's got a lot of extra that I can draw on. It'll take three of us all right. Where—and when?"

"Back to Larida's *residencia,* and as quickly as we can get going. Listen, Tony! If Larida has been left behind permanently, then we are badly bunkered. Brady will not return, but if Larida is going to join him, someone has got to return, and if they do they will almost certainly have rendezvous at the *residencia.* We may make Larida talk yet. But we won't count on that. So we'll wait at the *residencia.*"

"But we'll have to leave the Moth on the roof, and it would be seen when they return."

"That's a risk we've got to take. It is such a bold play that I'm hoping it will fool Brady. I want him to think that Larida has settled us as he planned, and that he had taken the Moth as part of his loot. If the Bat does return I'll see that Larida is on the roof in person to wave to it and give colour to my scheme. And," he added grimly, "if he plays any hanky-panky he'll need more help then Brady can give him."

RUSHTON would have had some diffidence against taking direct action against the *residencia* owing to it having so recently been a house of death, and, likewise, he would have been inclined to deal leniently with Larida (just as he had refused to press matters against Darrell Richfield) were it not for ample evidence that Larida was a murderous hound who cared not two jots about the death of his wife or of those poor deluded wretches in Barcelona.

As a matter of fact, Grant Rushton's suspicions were only too well founded. Never had Rushton sized up a situation more correctly.

From the moment of seeing the jealousy crazed countess lying on the floor, Larida's metamorphosis had been complete.

To him the necessary details regarding the funeral in the small plot of consecrated ground close to the chapel was merely a matter of form to be got through as quickly as possible.

Then he threw himself into Brady's plans with an enthusiasm which suited even the master-criminal, avid as he was for every peseta he could wring out of the bonds.

It was, indeed, his suggestion that Barcelona should be turned upside down so that dire confusion there should effectually blanket their movements.

"I'll be on the spot myself," he assured Brady. "If you are prepared to spend a few thousand pesetas, I can fix it for the *moufs* to take a hand."

Brady was interested in more ways than one.

"If we can get that fellow Grant Rushton—" he began.

"The *moufs* will get him if I can locate him. They haven't too much courage, and don't like the cold steel of the troops. But they'll settle your score with him. I go to Barcelona to complete the matter of the bonds. Say the word and I will arrange for an uprising in the city and for the *moufs* to come down the hill. I will also discover where this fellow Rushton is staying. And it may be that I shall be able to capture his aeroplane. If we go to the Riff country an extra 'plane would be a great asset."

Thinking of the sheik who still rode the Atlas valleys south of the Riff unsubdued by the French or Spaniards, Brady nodded vigorously.

"El Quayou would welcome such a gift, *amigo*. He is more modern than Abdel Krim. I like your suggestion. Let us see what we can do with it. How many thousand pesetas would turn the city upside down as you suggest?"

The result was what Grant Rushton and Tony had seen. And if the *moufs* had not been the arrant cowards, rats of the dark they are, the two detectives would never have got away alive from the hotel in the Rambla.

The attack on the hotel was no haphazard part of the march of the mob down the Rambla as they had at the time believed, although even then Rushton thought there was something very "prepared" and definite about it.

But Larida was right. The rats had no fancy for the sort of reception they met at the hands of Rushton, Tony, and the unknown Spaniard.

They did not know exactly whom they were to kill. They only knew they were to make wreckage of the hotel as they passed, and, with the number of dead and wounded they had left behind, they considered they had done their duty.

Larida's bribe money had already been dissipated, and the lure of chances for looting in the lower city was too strong to detain them at the hotel for very long.

Larida was dependable. When Brady and the other two had taken off, he lost no time in starting out to locate the Moth. It was when he was making a surveillance of the hangar from which he and Brady intended to steal the machine on Brady's return—he believed that Rushton and Tony were accounted for by now—that, to his amazement, those two individuals appeared on the scene.

So the facile Larida promptly decided to kill them then and there, knowing that the mob had failed.

So sure was he of his knowledge of the tangle of surrounding vegetation and his ability to dodge any risk of pursuit by the two Englishmen—he thought Grant Rushton very much overrated—that he had paid insufficient attention to his line of retreat.

The price he paid for this carelessness is known. And bitter thoughts did him no good as, doubled up like a half-filled sack of bran, he was carried in the Moth to his own *residencia,* a prisoner.

Of course, Rushton and Tony had no notion how many of Larida's own men might be at the place.

But Rushton was not worried too much on that score. He had seen the flat roof, and how one descended into the house. He knew that type of old Aragon architecture, and he figured that, with their automatics, he and Tony could put up a pretty stiff show of it once they landed.

He was to find that resistance was negligible, for during the latter period of Larida's residence there he had, as is known, been cut off from almost all association with his former friends in Barcelona.

What servants there were about the place were old family retainers, belonging to his late wife's side, and among them there were no more than three who could have made any effective resistance even if they would.

The waning moon was now well up in the night sky. There wasn't a cloud in the whole heavens. The air was cold, and, aside from the deep shadows in the valleys, the visibility was far clearer than would have been the case farther north under similar conditions.

Tony had no difficulty at all in making his goal. The *residencia* stood out, whiter and more distinct than ever under the white light.

The glow of Barcelona, far behind them, was entirely lost here in the effulgence of the moon. It was as though they were arriving at some uncharted spot in a strange world, so lonely and sentinel-like did the *residencia* appear.

Although the Moth was, strictly speaking, a two-seater, she made not the slightest trouble about her extra burden. Indeed, Tony never noticed the extra weight even when he banked steeply, and privily he was pleased at the chance to make the test, for, while Rushton didn't know it yet, he was planning to fix extra tanks later on, and attempt a certain long and difficult flight which he had had in his mind for a long time past.

He slid down towards the flat roof as smoothly as a gull dropping to the beach.

The moment the Moth taxied to a stop, Rushton was over the side. When he saw that the 'plane was all right, he signed to Tony to keep an eye on the prisoner, and, finding the trapdoor, caught hold of an iron ring that had been fitted to a heavy screw-bolt on the upper side.

It came up easily enough, revealing the shadowy beginning of the staircase beneath.

Rushton got out his pocket flashlight and automatic, and began to descend. He found the arrangement of the place much as he had figured, the narrow, enclosed staircases each dividing the mansion off into so many separate units, just as so many of the ancient *residencias* of Aragon and Castile were planned.

He reached the colonnaded balcony and began to walk its length. Most of the windows were closed, but the french windows of the main salon were open.

He stepped inside, and swept the light round slowly. There were plenty of signs that the room had been used recently, and, advancing to the big carved table in the centre, he found indications that a hurried meal had been made not long since, for there were used plates and the remains of a loaf of bread, part of a cold joint, the carcass of a chicken, and some empty country wine-bottles.

He counted the places used. Four.

"That might account for Brady, Gloria Ravissa, Liddle, and Larida," he thought. "It looks as if they partook of the meal just before leaving in the Bat. In that case there must be very few servants, or what there are must be very slack on the job for the remains to be left here all this time."

He stepped back on to the gallery and switched off the light. He told himself that it was odd that he had not seen a soul since he had arrived.

"It can't be that they are unaware of our arrival," he muttered as he stared down into the moon-washed patio. "They couldn't help but hear the 'plane. On the other hand, they may have thought it was the Bat, and they may have orders to remain in their quarters until summoned. I'll investigate, anyway. But first I'd better go back and have a word with Tony."

He ascended to the roof, where he found Tony leaning against the Moth, with one eye on Larida. He had found some wooden chocks that had been used for the Bat, and had put these under the wheels of the Moth; also he had pushed the Moth along into one corner, so that there would be plenty of clearance for the Bat to land if she returned.

Rushton nodded with approval.

"That's the stuff! Everything seems dead down below. I'm going to push farther and see what I turn out. You'd better remain here. I shan't be long."

"Suppose they're lying in ambush there?"

"I don't anticipate any trouble. I have a hunch that what servants there may be are not very effective."

"Hadn't we better have a signal?"

"If you hear a shot, come down."

"Okay."

Rushton descended the stairs once more and, on reaching the gallery this time, turned to the left.

He found what he expected—an outside flight of stairs leading down into the courtyard. He reached the cobbles and again stood listening. Not a sound did he hear.

He edged his way past the corner of the house, where the moonlight fell on the white cobbles without a thing to break it. Now it was almost as clear as day, and, putting his torch in his pocket, Rushton moved along towards where the white abode of the servants' quarters stood out against the dark of the vegetation behind.

As he crossed the bit of courtyard the pungent odour of smoke drifted to his nostrils, but he could see no plume against the sky.

The smell became stronger as he progressed, and when he reached the front of the quarters he paused again, for everything was still as quiet as the tomb.

Looking upwards towards the roof of the mansion, he could see the side coping plainly, but not Tony. Then he remembered that the lad would be on the other side, near where the trap opened.

He turned the corner of the servants' quarters, and now saw the cause of the smoke. There was a small pile of glowing coals in the open just ahead, and lying on the ground beside this was a human form.

Rushton approached still closer, and stirred the bundle with his toe. Instantly the form came to life, and Rushton drew back as it came erect. But at sight of the ancient, graven countenance that faced him he lowered his gun and spoke gently.

"Be not afraid, *hombre*. I intend you no harm. Where are the other servants?"

"They are all gone, senor—all gone," was the quavering answer. "None remain but old Juan, who has no place to go."

"All gone! What do you mean? Have they deserted, or did Count Larida send them away?"

"They were told by His Excellency to go as they wished, senor. His Excellency told us that now he would leave the *residencia* for a long time. He is returning, but to close it. He gave us a month's wages and dismissed us. But there is no place for old Juan to go. All my life, senor, have I been in the service of the family. I was born within these walls. I knew the late senora, rest her soul, when she was a mere *chiquita.* Where, then, is there for old Juan to go? You do not mean me harm, senor?"

"I mean you no harm," Rushton reassured him. "I shall be in the house for a day or two, but you need not fear. Your master is also here, and will remain for the same time. But you need not attend upon us. We shall look after ourselves. Do you understand?"

"*Si,* senor. I shall do whatever I am told."

"*Bueno.* Are the gates locked?"

"*Si,* senor."

"Then listen carefully. You are not to unlock them to anyone—to anyone at all! Do you understand?"

"Not even the padre, senor?"

"Not even the padre. Better still, I shall take the key. Where is it?"

"I shall bring it, senor."

The old man entered a door at the end of the quarters, and in a moment or two returned carrying an enormous old iron key, which he placed in Rushton's hands.

"There are no means of entry by the road?"

"None without that key, senor."

"Good! I shall keep it until we leave. You will remain here unless you are summoned. You have food for yourself?"

"Plenty, senor. There is enough for many days."

"And for us?"

"*Si,* senor. His Excellency knows where it is kept."

"Very well. That is all."

Rushton turned and went round the end of the adobe building, well pleased with his investigations. If the old man was telling the truth—and he had no reason to suppose he could be lying—then his rear was well guarded.

With no effectiveness among the servants to start a counter-offensive, and no chance of anyone getting in through the gates, he and Tony could concentrate on what might come by air.

Returning to the roof, he and Tony got the cramped Larida out of the cockpit. They carried him down the stairs to the gallery, and only then did Rushton remove the gag.

While Larida was held propped in a chair in the salon by Tony, Rushton talked to him in Spanish.

"You know who we are, Larida, so we needn't waste any time on introductions. Now I want you to get straight what I have to say. I know what sort of a stunt you pulled off in Barcelona to-night. You and Brady have worked a big ramp here, and Brady has made a good get-away. I know where he has gone all right, and I know that he's got to come back for you—unless he gives you the double-cross. So we are going to wait right here for his return, and if you behave yourself you will fare as comfortably as my assistant and I. I have already investigated the servants' quarters. There isn't anyone left but old Juan. You sent them away too soon. And no one will get in by the gates, because I hold the key."

He held up the big iron key as he spoke.

"I'm saying nothing now about your attempt to murder me this evening, Larida. We shall come to that later. For the present everything hinges on Brady. Everything is to be subordinated to his return. If you wish to indicate any particular room which will be large enough to accommodate all three of us, it may save time. If not, then we shall find one ourselves."

But Larida would not talk. He simply rolled his head and cursed thickly, so, with a shrug, Rushton turned from him.

"Keep an eye on him, young 'un. I'll soon find a room that will serve our purpose."

He made good his word, and within a quarter of an hour they were encamped with their prisoner in an enormous old room up near the roof, prepared to wait until Brady should open the next act, or, failing to appear on the scene, should force Rushton to write finis and failure to this case, in which, so far, Brady had taken most of the tricks.

DURING the time of Abdel Krim, when "Flash" Brady had been his confidant, captain of his first-line troops, and known to the French and Spaniards, as well as the savage mountain Riff tribes, as Sakr-el-Droog—Hawk of the Peak—there could be no question about his welcome in the mountain stronghold.

But many snows had mantled the top of the Atlas Mountains since the French had taken Abdel Krim to life-long exile in Madagascar, and the once dreaded Riffians were now no more feared than some degenerate tribe who did nothing more warrior-like than tend its flocks.

Not that there had not been outbursts of revolt against the domination of the Spaniards and French. But these had been sporadic affairs, due to lack of leadership.

Nevertheless, it would take more than one generation to turn the Riffian into a woman, as the saying in those parts goes, and had not Abdel Krim the Lion of the Riff—been taken, a vast number more of French and Spaniards would have found a grave beneath the sands of North Africa before the tribe was driven back upon itself.

Since then no leader of note had appeared. Once or twice Brady had been in contact with the tribe, but nothing much had come of it.

Nevertheless, he had more than once toyed with the idea of going back and becoming their war chieftain, this idea finding most prominence in his thoughts when the police were hottest on his trail.

Not for some time past, however, had he had any contact with the men of the hills, and when he decided, after the most successful coup he had ever got away with, to seek sanctuary there, he knew perfectly well that he was taking a risk.

But Brady was always a gambler, and he told himself that at last his star was in the ascendant, with Lady Luck sitting on his shoulder.

Close on to half a million sterling he had nipped right out from under Grant Rushton's nose. There wasn't another crook at large who could have done that, he exulted to Gloria Ravissa.

And not only had he made a clean getaway with the bonds from Fingest, but, in Barcelona, he had checkmated Rushton a second time.

It was, to Brady, far more than the discount he had accepted just to see Rushton chasing himself round in circles.

Certainly it looked as if he had some ground to boast. Things had not begun too auspiciously at Larida's *residencia*; but, thanks to the promptitude with which Gloria Ravissa had acted, that obstacle had been permanently and swiftly removed.

He knew before he left the 'drome at Barcelona on the night of the riot that Larida had done his part well.

He had given the Moth the slip nicely. He had zoomed into the air and headed for North Africa knowing that Larida was behind to carry out their murderous purpose on Rushton if the *moufs* in the city failed to click.

And with him went a stack of good peseta money that was just as good for his purpose as sterling.

He already had in mind the place where he would land when they were across the Mediterranean and the Straits of Gibraltar.

This was well beyond the French and Spanish outposts, well up among the foothills of the northern spur of the Atlas, a wide platform which he had prepared as an emergency landing-ground during the days of Abdel Krim, and which he figured would still be possible now, for it would scarcely be overgrown sufficiently to matter, the herbage on those slopes being stunted enough at any time.

He knew, however, that it would be necessary to carry enough petrol and oil to make the return journey, for there would be no chance of procuring supplies in that desolate spot.

About two miles distant he hoped to find one of the villages he had known still inhabited by the Riffs. If so, he had little doubt of his welcome. If they had abandoned it, and it was either deserted or occupied by some less warlike tribe, then he would have to manage through what conditions suggested when he got there.

It would be essential for him to arrange immediately for the safety of Gloria Ravissa. It wasn't only her person that must be safeguarded, but all the loot he was taking along, for that must remain with her while he returned for Larida.

There was, of course, a great temptation to desert Larida and leave him to stew in his own juice.

It was through no spirit of loyalty that Brady was intending to fly back with Liddle and pick him up. It was because Larida would fit into the plans he was forming for the future.

He knew perfectly well that Europe and America would be too hot to hold him for a long time to come—that is, unless he remained continually under cover; and that prospect did not suit Brady when he had such a terrific wad of money as now lay at his feet in the Bat.

Where else could he sit so freely as in the Riff? Nowhere. Where else would he be looked up to as a power? Nowhere. The name of Sakr-el-Droog was still worth something in the Riff.

And with nearly half a million sterling as reserve capital a lot might be done under those conditions and surroundings. The Riffs might be reorganised as an efficient fighting unit to harass the French and Spaniards once more.

With his money he could equip them with rifles and ammunition, and he'd get back his outlay through raids on desert caravans, and looting the outpost towns and villages of the French and Spaniards.

Here was where Larida would come in useful. Those guns could be run across from Barcelona, and that end of it could be organised by the Catalan, who knew every turn and twist of intrigue in that part of Spain.

Therefore the Bat must return for Larida.

Liddle, with strict instructions to fly with utmost care and regard for his fuel, made the journey in as direct a line as possible.

They flew all through the night without incident. Indeed, in their seats both Brady and Gloria Ravissa dozed for a great part of the way.

They crossed the African coast the next morning over a desolate sandy stretch that lay between the Spanish zone and the French colony of Algeria.

Liddle was flying very high, at more than three thousand feet. This was a safeguard, for, farther along the Zone, there were some Spanish scouting 'planes that Brady wished to avoid.

Very soon after they got their first glimpse of the northern spurs of the Atlas.

Up to now Liddle had been flying by dead reckoning, but from this point Brady took over the duties of navigator, for the master-criminal had flown all over that area in the past, and knew the layout of the plains and mountains beneath like the palm of his own hand.

From this point, too, Brady kept a close watch on the petrol-gauge. He knew what they would need for the return. He knew that sufficiency might mean all the difference between success and failure, for if they had to descend in some part of Spain for refuelling before they reached Barcelona, they might well find that Grant Rushton had been busy sending warning telegrams all over the country.

Brady knew that Rushton might make a pretty shrewd guess as to his intentions; but he was hoping devoutly that, long ere this, Rushton and Tony had been killed either by the mob or Larida.

A faint nostalgia stirred him as they drew nearer and nearer to the mountains. He was, above, everything, an adventurer, and he was not forgetting the stirring times he had had in this very country, nor that, farther south in Morocco, he had first met Gloria Ravissa.

She, too, must have been thinking of that night when the thousands of pilgrims crowded the hot desert town, of the pungent odour of the camels that rose on the dust-laden air of the dim harem into which she had lured the tall Arab (Brady was there in Arab dress) to seek his aid. And Brady showed his white teeth now in a smile as he read her thoughts.

Who would have thought that the famous Parisian dancer, the "Bird of Paradise," would have linked fate with that notorious criminal, "Flash" Brady, in a far-away walled town in the Moroccan desert?

Yet it had come to pass, and here they were again above the same sands, seeking sanctuary.

Liddle knew nothing of this. He was a crook, but he was only an unimportant cog in Brady's machine. He was also a good airman, and he was flying the Bat with more steadiness than speed in order to conserve his petrol, as instructed.

It was Brady who first spotted the valley which he sought. He touched Liddle's arm and pointed.

The 'plane came round a trifle, which made a wide arc that brought them to the mouth of the valley.

Here Brady pointed again. On the other side of the valley was a spur, showing green at this time of the year; and when Liddle had changed direction once more, Brady was certain he could sight the brown rectangle that should mark the landing-place he had in mind.

Suddenly, as a cleft in the spur opened out, Brady could see a village that, in the past, had been occupied by the Riffians. It was impossible to tell from this great height who might be occupying it now; but that human beings lived there was plain, for straight up into the morning air were climbing several thin plumes of smoke.

He pointed to the patch of brown, and signed for Liddle to make his landing there.

Immediately Liddle began to drop, steeply, swiftly, shooting his guns as he did so and letting the machine volplane under her own dive, so to speak.

He touched earth, ran along through short, wiry brown grass for a little distance, and then came to a stop with the petrol indicator showing just under half of the total tankage used since they had taken the air at Barcelona.

There was enough to get them back with a small margin for emergencies and possible head winds. But that margin was dangerously small.

Not a soul was in sight. From their eminence they could look right over the flank of the spur and along the full length of the valley.

Here and there lean, black-footed goats chewed the scant herbage, and overhead a single buzzard wheeled against the dead blue. But of humans not a sign.

But that, Brady knew, meant nothing. At this moment many pairs of eyes might be watching them, for no fox can take cover more effectively than a Riffian among the rocky fastnesses.

Brady stepped into full view, and, turning towards Mecca, made an obeisance such as would be the duty of any good Mussulman. Then he sent up his voice in a great shout that had echoed among those same hills in the days of Abdel Krim. If any Riffians were within earshot they must recognise that cry.

For a time nothing happened. Perhaps ten minutes went by. Then suddenly, where there had been a shoulder of plain grey stone, an armed man appeared magically.

He stood gazing at them in silence, leaning upon the barrel of his long rifle. His eyes were fixed on Brady, and Brady stood staring back.

He made another sign, and spoke rapidly in the tongue of the country. He used the name of Abdel Krim, and then spoke of himself as "Hawk of the Peak."

The man listened without reply. Then he vanished as swiftly as he had come. Brady shrugged, lit a cigarette, and walked back to the 'plane.

"It is in the lap of the gods now," he told Gloria Ravissa. "I don't know whether that fellow was a Riffian or not. But we shall soon know what sort of a reception we are to get. He will be gone to the village we saw. It must be about two miles away."

They waited, Liddle ready to take off again quickly in case of an attack. Brady smoked cigarette after cigarette, his eyes glued on the rock where the mountain man had first appeared.

Half an hour passed. An hour went by. And then another apparition was revealed against the rock.

But this individual was very different from the one they had seen before. He was dressed in the full garb of a sheik, and, instead of a straggly wisp on the chin, his beard was long and black, and cut into a fork, just as Brady used to wear his when running with Abdel Krim.

He and the other stared at each other for a full minute. Then Brady uttered a low cry of satisfaction.

"Abd-el-Kadr!" he shouted. "It is I, Sakr-el-Droog!"

The tall Riffian came forward slowly. No emotion showed in his black eyes, but before reaching Brady he laid his rifle on the grass.

Then they made greeting, and as their hands touched the rocks behind suddenly came alive with men.

Their voices rose in a great shout:

"Sakr-el-Droog! Sakr-el-Droog! Sakr-el-Droog has come back!"

Brady knew that Abd-el-Kadr was a nephew of Abdel Krim. He had known him when he was younger, and remembered him as a brave enough warrior, though without the executive ability necessary to weld the Riffians into the fighting effectiveness to which he and Abdel Krim had brought them.

But it was evident that he was inclined to be friendly, and there was no doubt about the honesty of the welcome the tribe generally was giving to the Hawk of the Peak.

When those formalities were over Brady took Abd-el-Kadr aside. Briefly he told him that he was inclined to return to the Riff, and to assume any position which it pleased Abd-el-Kadr to allot him.

"As I worked for the great Abdel Krim, so am I prepared to work for you, Abd-el-Kadr," he said. "Nor do I come empty-handed. You will remember how it was I who made possible the bringing in of arms and ammunition. I am ready to do that again, and it may be that the day will come before long when they will be useful against the *gaiours*"

"I have dreamed of such a day, Sakr-el-Droog," admitted the tall Riffian. "But things are not the same since the great Abdel Krim put the *gaiours* to flight. If you come you will be welcome. But I, Abd-el-Kadr, remain chief of the tribe."

"It must not be otherwise," returned Brady smoothly, confident that, once he got his feet in, he would soon get control of things. "My desire is to serve humbly under thee, Abd-el-Kadr."

There was much feasting in the village that day. Sakr-el-Droog was received back into the tribe, and sat on the right hand of Abd-el-Kadr.

Gloria Ravissa, even though a *gaiour* woman, was, of course, not present. But one of the largest houses in the village had been placed at her disposal, and in her care was the sack containing the stack of Spanish money which Brady had received for the stolen bonds.

It is little wonder, therefore, that when Brady and Liddle took the air again after midnight that night, when the waning moon was just showing above the desert to the east, that the master-criminal should smile to himself in triumph.

Not a hitch. He couldn't have planned for things to fall better than they had fallen.

"Flash" Brady was certainly getting the breaks.

CHAPTER XVII   WAITING

DURING the day and night following their arrival at Larida's *residencia* Grant Rushton and Tony lay very much doggo.

Rushton knew that, if his calculations were correct, then Brady could not put in an appearance before the second morning at least.

He knew there would be a certain amount of inevitable delay after Brady landed.

He did not know, of course, how soon Brady would be able to make direct contact with his former friends among the Riffians; nor could he guess whether Brady would make contact at all.

He knew it was quite on the cards that Brady might have in mind some spot where he could land, hide his loot, leave Gloria Ravissa and either send Liddle back alone for Larida, or come with him.

If the former proved to be the case, then Rushton realised there was nothing for it but for him and Tony to take care of Liddle and make the flight to Africa after forcing from Liddle a confession as to Brady's whereabouts.

But Rushton was hoping that Brady's desire to know as quickly as possible his fate and Tony's would cause him to make the return journey with Liddle.

Also, it was more than probable that there would be certain details of business and private matters to attend to before leaving Spain finally—that is, if, as Rushton figured, Brady was planning to spend some considerable time in the safety of the Riff.

It was useless to question Larida. He knew nothing definite. The whole thing hinged on Brady's movements; and Rushton did not fool himself for a single moment that, even if Brady did return, he would bring the money with him.

That had gone with him, and it would be his first duty to salt it down safely.

But Rushton was not crossing that bridge until he reached it. Let him get his hands on Brady and he would then solve the problem of the money.

Not a soul had come to the gates during their brief tenancy. Old Juan pottered about by himself in the servants' quarters, and Rushton and Tony found sufficient food in the place to keep them going.

From the roof Tony spotted an occasional mountain peasant who glanced at the huge pile fearfully as he passed, but for the most part the peasants gave the place a wide berth. Rushton and Tony were glad, then, that it was held in such sinister awe, for it left them undisturbed.

Nor was there any sign of the local padre, while the servants whom Larida had dismissed had apparently scattered among their homes.

Larida gave no trouble. Nor was he given a chance. He was given food and drink at regular intervals, and always either Rushton or Tony had him in sight.

They also took regular spells of watching from the roof, but it was not until the second evening—that would be the one following their arrival—that the gaze of each quickened with keenness as he peered into the sky.

It was that same evening that Rushton had a talk with Larida.

"I'm going to give you a chance to talk, Larida," he said. "I don't for a moment think you will do so, or, if you do, you will probably lie. That doesn't make any difference. You are going to get the chance. Do you want to say anything?"

Larida shook his head.

"I've got nothing to say to you!" he snarled. "But when I get out of this I'll settle with you for what you've done!"

"You're not out of it yet, my fine fellow. And, as for a settlement, it is not likely to go the way you wish. I've got one to make with you for trying to blow my head off."

"Why don't you hand me over to the Barcelona police, then?"

Rushton grinned at him.

"You'd like that, wouldn't you, you murderous little rat? That's exactly what I am not going to do. I know how long you'd remain in custody there. I've got methods of my own. But you are of little importance. It is Brady who engages my attention."

"And a lot of good that will do you!" sneered Larida. "He's beaten you on every turn of the game, and he'll leave you stranded at the last."

"Well, if he does he'll leave you high and dry beside me," was Rushton's cool response.

"He'll get me out of this all right," asserted Larida confidently.

Rushton pricked up his ears. In those words he seemed to read a definite hint that Brady would be returning with the 'plane.

Rushton leaned over and gripped Larida's shoulder with such

142

violence that the other gasped with the pain.

"You don't want to talk, so I will!" he snarled. "Now listen to me. You can pull off a good many stunts here in Catalonia. I know something about what goes on. But Brady is my meat, and I'm going to get him. Murder in England is a very different thing from what it is out here."

"Then why don't you go after him in the usual way?" demanded Larida. "Why don't your police take a hand? What about the police of Barcelona? You haven't got any more official standing here than Brady. You've got no authority to charge him, let alone arrest him."

"I didn't say I was going to arrest him. The police of England can take their own course to apprehend him on the murder charge. I'm after something else, and I'll get it."

"You'll have a long, dry journey," jeered Larida.

"When I get it the stuff will be laid in my hands," Rushton assured him. "But you and I will keep to cases. Brady will come back for you. And he'll find you waiting just as he expects."

Larida's eyes narrowed.

"What are you up to now?" he demanded.

"You're going to welcome him, my fine fellow. You'll be on the roof when he shows up, and you'll give him a wave. That is what is appointed for you, and if you try any tricks, then heaven help you!"

"And if I refuse?"

"Of course you'll refuse. I've figured on that. But you won't keep it up long. I'm going to give you a taste of the medicine you and Brady would give me or Tony if the positions were reversed. You can think that over."

With that Rushton went to find Tony.

"We'll have to take sharp measures with Larida, my lad. If he gets a chance he'll queer our pitch."

"They'll have to be stiff ones, then, chief."

"They will!" snapped Rushton savagely. "I'm not going to risk having him wreck everything now. We've got to get Brady—we've got to get him! I'll show you what we'll do to Larida when the moment comes."

Their watch was much more intense during that night. From the time when Rushton knew it was a bare possibility for Brady to be making an appearance—that is, calculating the time for a return journey without any allowance for a stop-over—one of them was always on the roof.

Dawn came without any signs of the Bat.

Rushton was really not expecting Brady so soon. On the other hand, he was taking no chances of a surprise.

At ten o'clock, leaving Tony on watch over Larida and the roof, he descended to the ground, and went along to the servants' quarters.

Old Juan was, as usual, pottering about, and when Rushton demanded a charcoal brazier he brought one from the kitchen lean-to. It was almost full of glowing coals, which was exactly what Rushton required.

He carried this up into the house and mounted the stairs to the room. Tony regarded the brazier in a puzzled way.

"What's the idea? Are we going to do some cooking up here?"

Rushton smiled grimly.

"Some cooking—yes, possibly. Go down and bring Larida, young 'un."

With his curiosity still unsatisfied, Tony went to obey. Presently he reappeared, forcing Larida in front of him.

Rushton waited until they reached the top, then he indicated the third step down.

"Now, listen, Larida," he said curtly. You are to stand on the third step. Bind his ankles again, Tony."

Tony obeyed.

"Your arms will now be released," went on Rushton. "On that step your body will be partially exposed through the trap and plainly visible to Brady if he approaches in the 'plane. When you see him, if he does come, you are to wave to him as if everything was all right. Do you understand?"

"And if I refuse?" snarled Larida.

"You are going to get a cooking, my fine fellow. Take off his shoes and socks, Tony."

Tony, seeing now what was in Rushton's mind, had those bits of gear off in a twinkling.

"Some cooking, I said, Larida," he heard Rushton's cold voice repeating. "I am going to place this brazier on the step beneath you. My assistant and I are going to be there, too. I am going to watch through the trap with a gun against your thigh. My assistant is going to keep hold of your ankles, and if you try any tricks I shall give him a sign. If I do give that sign one of your naked feet is going to be pushed into the red-hot coals in this brazier. It won't be after you have played your trick. It will be at the first sign I detect. So now you know. Get ready, young 'un. We shall begin our real watch now."

It was, however, not for another two hours or so that their expectations looked like being realised.

Then it was Tony's ear that first caught the faint sound that was like the buzzing of some insect.

The lad knew, however, that it came from an aeroplane. Rushton had heard it now, and, signing to Tony to keep a sharp eye on Larida, he pushed through the trap so he could look away to the south.

There, far in the clear blue, he saw something that looked like a gull speeding towards them. But he knew it for the Bat, and when there could no longer be any doubt that it was coming towards the *residencia*, he withdrew, giving a final warning to Larida as he did so.

There was nothing to do now but wait.

The drone of the machine reached them more and more distinctly. All of them, even Larida, stared up through the trap in suppressed excitement, for all three knew that on the next few minutes hung a terrific chance.

Once they saw the machine, now quite close, swoop across their line of vision.

Rushton and Tony knew that Liddle would be banking immediately after in order to jockey into position for the landing.

They waited tensely, listening for the tell-tale cessation of sound that would tell them when he had shot his gun.

It came. They stiffened. Rushton jammed the muzzle of the weapon into Larida's thigh. Tony tightened his grip on Larida's ankles. Then Rushton hissed:

"Now, now—wave, you crook, and do it naturally, or you'll sizzle! On with it!"

Larida hesitated. Had he for one second believed Rushton was bluffing he would, even under the threat, have tried to convey some warning to Brady.

He knew it was his ally now. As he stood, half in and half out of the trap, he could see the 'plane distinctly, could even make out the two heads of the men in the cockpit.

But he was certain there was no bluffing about the man who had grabbed him so swiftly outside the hangar. And, moreover, he was anxious for his own sake to have Brady on the scene. He told himself that, with both Brady and Liddle, they would soon find means to settle Rushton and Tony.

So he waved a welcome to the plane that was swooping downwards towards the roof.

And, as soon as he had done so, Rushton hauled him bodily down through the trap and hustled him to the bottom of the stairs.

"Come on, Tony. Bring the brazier."

Tony grabbed the brazier, and followed. Rushton had opened the first door on his right—a disused bedroom.

He flung Larida to the floor, and, just as the Catalan opened his mouth to yell, Rushton clapped his hand hard against his teeth.

While Tony retied his arms, Rushton gagged him, and they had just finished the job when Tony, stepping out on to the small landing, saw the shadow of the Bat above the trap.

He withdrew into the room, and, with guns drawn, the pair stood waiting.

They could hear the double thud on the roof when Brady and Liddle came out of the cockpit. Then the murmur of voices reached them, while footsteps moved backwards and forwards across the roof. They knew that the pair above were examining the Moth, and debating how Larida had got it where it was.

Then a voice came roaring down the staircase. It was Brady's.

"Larida!"

Rushton glanced at Tony with warning. For a second time the summons came.

"Larida!"

Still the pair inside the door half-way down stood tensely waiting. A brief silence and then voices again. They could hear now distinctly.

"Where the devil has he got to?" they heard Brady grumbling. "He was here a minute ago."

A reply which they knew must be Liddle's said:

"Maybe he's getting his gear together."

"Well, he'd better get a move on. We want to leave at once and get refuelled. Larida!"

He shouted the name again as he came clumping down the stairs. Rushton and Tony couldn't tell whether he was first with Liddle following or whether the positions were reversed. They could only wait.

Again and again Brady roared Larida's name and, happening to turn, Rushton was just in time to see Larida lifting his bound feet to drum with his heels on the floor.

He took a swift stride and planted a kick in the Catalan's ribs that caused him to change his mind swiftly. There was no place here for squeamishness. Life and death hung on the next few minutes.

Rushton was back in position when the first person descending the stairs reached the landing and continued down. They stood until the second was just past then Rushton jerked open the door and leaped on to the little landing.

"Brady, stick 'em up!"

Brady was about four steps from the bottom and Liddle just a few steps beneath Rushton at the moment of this tableau. Tony was close to Rushton, his gun sticking under Rushton's uplifted arm.

Brady turned at the sound of his name. He knew Rushton's voice well enough. He stood staring in disbelief for a long moment, it seemed, then, with an oath, he went for his gun.

Rushton shot as Brady threw himself headlong towards the opening that gave on to the gallery. Liddle had crouched, frozen, until the crash of Rushton's weapons released him.

He gave a cry and dived for the bottom.

Crack, crack, crack!

Rushton, Tony and Brady fired on almost the same instant. It was Tony's shot that caught Liddle and sent him tumbling in a heap to the bottom.

The enclosed space of the staircase became filled with smoke. Rushton and Tony saw Brady weaving about as a blur in the fog. The racketing of the guns was appalling with no outlet for the waves of sound.

The blur that had been Brady disappeared. Rushton and Tony tumbled down the stairs, leaping Liddle's prostrate body.

Out on the gallery they got a fleeting glimpse of Brady, who flung a shot at them just before he disappeared into one of the rooms.

The two detectives rushed along until they came to the open windows of the salon. Brady was not there.

They rushed back to the gallery and moved along cautiously. Neither was absolutely certain into which room Brady had gone.

They peered into the next. It was in a state of confusion, but Brady was not there. They advanced still farther, towards the rooms that had formed the private apartments of the late countess.

It was the loud slamming of a door that brought them up with a jerk. They heard Brady's voice in the near distance. He was cursing and calling upon Larida, threatening what he would do if he found him. It was evident that Brady believed Larida had betrayed him.

Rushton and Tony started back just as Brady, burst out on to the gallery between them and the salon. From this, it was plain that he must have found his way from one room to another, thus placing himself closer to the staircase leading to the roof than Rushton and Tony now stood.

He turned his curses upon them, shooting savagely as he roared. He seemed quite reckless of whether their bullets got him or not and, indeed, it was a miracle that he escaped, for both detectives were shooting fast.

Brady turned and ran once more. They saw him dash into the opening of the staircase leading to the roof, heard his voice again as he stumbled over Liddle, then came the heavy clatter of his feet as he went up the stairs.

"He'll give us the slip yet," jerked Rushton. "Come on; we've got to stop him."

For his part, Brady was already up to the small landing. Rushton and Tony had left open the door of the room where they had been waiting and now, as he passed, Brady must have seen Larida lying bound and gagged.

But he did not attempt to rescue him. Just as he had left Liddle lying where he had fallen so did he abandon Larida to his fate.

It was plain enough now to the master criminal what had happened, and how Rushton had fooled him on his arrival. But he still had a strong card to play. He was between Rushton and the trap that led to the roof.

He was flying up the last section of the stairs as Rushton and Tony leaped Liddle's body and started after him.

Plunging through the trap, Brady whirled round and emptied his weapon at the pair, the bullet thudding into stairs and walls close to them as they jerked this way and that in their ascent.

Brady slammed down the trap and leaped towards the Bat. He had something definite in his mind for his hand went up at once to a strip of wood that lay on the bottom of the cockpit.

Another leap took him back to the trap and, thrusting the wood down close to the edge of the trap, he used the butt of his pistol as a hammer.

At best, it made only a temporary wedge, but Brady was fighting for periods of time where seconds would be as precious as drops of gold.

When he could hammer the wedge in no farther he rushed once more to the Bat and hauled himself into the cockpit. Taking the stick, he shot the gun and pressed the starter.

For tense, vital moments it could be heard grinding until the engine gave a sudden roar and then with a backward glance at the trap, Brady put the Bat straight along the roof towards the end where Larida had removed the parapet so that a 'plane might take off.

Had he started from the other end he would have had a run and to spare. But so short was the run he took that, when the Bat slid over the edge it looked as if it would nose dive straight to the cobbles beneath.

But Brady held her steady, easing her up and up until she began to climb. It was a miracle that he cleared some trees by the chapel; it was a greater miracle that he was able to bank and bring her to a still higher level. Then he flattened her out and, as he zoomed away eastwards, he lifted one fist and shook it, yelling at the top of his lungs:

"Stew, you hound, stew. You'll never catch me now."

It was at this moment that Rushton and Tony managed to burst through the wedged trap-door. With both of them under it, the trap gave with such violence when the wedge was driven out, that it hit the roof with sufficient force to smash the hinges.

Scrambling out on to the roof they saw the Bat just clear of the trees. With one accord they turned and raced for the Moth. Tony hauled it round and Rushton scrambled in.

Tony gave the propeller a whir and the engine roared. He raced round and threw himself in. Rushton, who had been handling the instruments, sliding back to give him room.

Then Tony set the Moth to the run, having the whole length of the roof ahead of him for, it will be remembered, he had hauled the Moth along into one corner in preparation for Brady's arrival.

Both were thinking the same thing. Unless Brady had stopped somewhere on the way back for petrol then he could not possibly have more than enough to take him a very short distance.

Would he make for Barcelona? Or would he deem that too risky?

For his part, Brady was already thinking about the same problem. So engrossed had he been in making his getaway that the thought of his diminished store of petrol did not occur to him until he was aloft.

Then he saw the tell-tale arrow in the gauge. Not more than enough to take him two score miles or so.

Barcelona was ruled out as too risky. No matter whether Rushton was making use of orthodox police powers or not, he would soon be able to put a crimp in his tail if he caught him on the landing ground at Barcelona.

Then where? He could not, dared not try to make Madrid. He must find a place near for the situation was truly desperate.

He remembered Sitjes, along the sandy coast from Barcelona. If he could land there he could get supplies.

He did not know yet whether the Moth was in pursuit or not. But he knew the risk of that, and he cursed again as he thought how remiss he had been not to put the other machine out of commission before he left.

He altered his course a little towards the southeast. Where Barcelona was about fifty miles from the *residencia,* Sitjes would be about forty. He might just about make it.

He knew when he turned around presently that the Moth was after him. But the Bat had more speed, he flattered himself—he was mistaken there— and he let it all out. It didn't matter now how fast the petrol went if he could only cover those forty miles.

He turned several times to see the other machine against the blue. Tony was flying on about the same level, and Brady frowned as he noticed that it appeared somewhat larger than before. Could the Moth be overtaking him? Impossible!

He debated what he should do if they landed at Sitjes. It would mean shooting it out to a finish. And, leaving the Bat to pilot herself for a little, he saw to his loading.

Then the Mediterranean lay before him with the sandy line of the coast. He saw the flat roofs and white buildings of Sitjes. He grinned savagely as he looked back once more. And then a mighty curse burst from him as the engine coughed warningly.

That cough developed into a rapid stuttering that told its own tale. The tank was empty. The Bat was using the last drops.

He stared ahead desperately for a place to land. He was now

almost directly over the beach about a mile from Sitjes. But he could not make Sitjes now. He must make a forced landing as best he could.

He shot his gun and began to slide earthwards. He had his eye on a sandy stretch that looked flat enough for his purpose.

The sand was bumpier than it had appeared from above, but he landed well enough. By the time the Bat lurched to a stop against a miniature dune, Brady was out of the cockpit, his gun in hand.

Up above, the Moth was coming down in a long glide. Without waiting for her to land, Brady began to shoot.

He figured that Tony would touch ground as close to the Bat as possible, but the lad, at a sign from Rushton, had lifted his machine a little and, shooting past the Bat, came to the sand some forty yards farther on.

By the time Rushton reached the ground Brady was coming towards him on the run, shooting as he came. It was safe enough there on that desolate stretch. Not another soul was in sight.

And, this time, Rushton was determined that there should be no further escape.

He allowed Brady to haul away at the trigger, holding his own fire while the bullets kicked up the sand all about him.

He knew that Tony was running towards him, but he paid no attention to anything. He stood immobile until Brady came within the range he had set himself.

Then he shot, as coolly as if he were on the range.

There was no confusion here to upset his aim. There was just the deliberate pulling of the trigger at that figure rushing towards him.

And Grant Rushton was no mean marksman. He proved it then, for on the crashing of Rushton's weapon, Brady pulled up as if some giant, invisible hand had grasped him. He stood rocking on his heels for a few moments, then he pitched face down on to the sand.

"Where did you get him?" Rushton heard Tony gasp at his shoulder.

"Through the thigh just as I intended. But watch him. He can crawl to his gun. Come on."

They raced along the sand just as Brady's fingers were clawing at the weapon that had jerked clear of his grasp as he fell. Tony landed both feet on his wrist, bending down to retrieve the weapon as he did so.

Rushton was already bending over him and, proving to his own satisfaction that he had made a hit where he had told Tony, he straightened up.

"I'll watch him, Tony. Take the Moth and land at Sitjes. Get some petrol in tins. It will do for the time being. Then I'll fly Brady back in the Bat while you bring the Moth."

"Back—where, chief?"

"To the *residencia*. This thing isn't finished yet."

CHAPTER XVIII   RUSHTON'S TERMS

BUT it was, nearly.

Nevertheless, no one could realise better than Rushton that there were still many complications ahead.

On the other hand, he had "Flash" Brady in his power, not handicapped by any duty he owed to the police, but his own prisoner, with his own prison in which to keep him.

And Rushton was determined that in that prison he should remain until he had secured what he had come after.

Tony's arrival on the sands at Sitjes created a certain amount of curiosity, and, following his packing of half a dozen petrol tins in the cockpit and taking off, a string of inquisitive persons began running along the sands. It was as if they guessed without seeing that something had happened farther along.

But by the time they came trailing into sight the tins had been emptied into the Bat's tank, and, with the wounded Brady bound in the cockpit, Rushton was already in the air.

Tony lifted the Moth off the sands soon after, allowing Rushton to leave him some distance behind so that he should have plenty of time for landing on the roof of the *residencia.*

By the time Tony came down Rushton had already carried his prisoner below and laid him on a bed. Then they went to work on the wound, which, Rushton thought, was not going to present any great trouble, for the bullet had gone through clean.

Not until that job was done did he draw up a chair, light a cigarette, and broach to Brady the thing that had to be settled.

"Well," he said quietly, "that's that. Now, what about things, Brady?"

Brady, who was quite conscious, favoured him with a curse.

"That isn't going to get you any place, my bucko," returned Rushton. "I'm holding the cards this hand, and the whole thing depends on whether you are going to play out your hand or give me trick and game. I've got you cold on the Richfield job, Brady, and, just so you won't think I'm bluffing, I'll tell you how it was done."

Slowly and methodically, just as at the inquest, Rushton told the story he had formed from the theory built up from each little item of evidence he had found. And had he needed confirmation he found it in the expression in Brady's agate-coloured eyes.

When he had finished Brady did not speak at once. When he did so, it was to ask for a drink, and Rushton fetched a carafe of country brandy.

He then gave him a cigarette, for he could see that his nerves were on the ragged edge. When Brady had smoked a quarter of it he twisted his head a little.

"Well, what are you going to do? You can't take me back to England without proper proceedings, and you won't get much satisfaction there—in this part of Spain."

"Don't you fool yourself. I'd get you back to England if I wanted you there. But that is Scotland Yard's baby. Let them see to it. I want something else, and I'm going to get it, or believe me or not, you are coming with me just the same."

"What is it?"

"Two things. Firstly, I want the gun with which you killed Mrs. Richfield."

"Why?"

"I need it. That's enough. It isn't going to alter your position one iota if I have it."

"What else?"

"The money, of course."

"I haven't got it."

"Don't take me for an infant. I know you have it well salted away in the Riff country."

"Safe from you."

"And you. If you leave Gloria Ravissa out there with a wad like that, you'll never see her or the money again. You're due for a long term or the rope, if I land you back in England."

"And if I agreed to your terms?"

"I'll leave you here. But I'll notify the Barcelona police and also Scotland Yard."

Brady grinned.

"The Barcelona gang are nuts," he sneered.

"You may slip up on that one of these days. But which is it? Do you give me a letter which I shall want? I'm not haggling with you. It is all or nothing, and don't waste my time. If I go out to the Riff I'm starting to-night. On the other hand, Tony flies into Barcelona with messages for Scotland Yard and the Barcelona police. Take your choice."

"Will you bring Gloria Ravissa back here?"

"If she wishes to come. But it must be distinctly understood that there is no hanky-panky. I shall leave Tony on guard here, with strict instructions what to do in case I have not returned in a reasonable time."

"And Liddle and Larida?"

Rushton turned to Tony.

"What about Liddle, young 'un?"

"He's all right. I've just been down. My bullet got him in the head, but it isn't dangerous. I've fixed him up and tied him, to be on the safe side."

"Liddle and Larida get the same treatment as you, Brady," said Rushton curtly. "If you can bamboozle the police after I leave, that is up to you. But I want that money—every peseta that you got."

"All right," growled Brady, with slow regret, "I agree."

. . . . . .

Abd-el-Kadr and almost every effective fighting man in the tribe was on the primitive landing-ground on the spur of the Atlas when the returning Bat showed in the dead blue of the sky to the north.

Although it was against tribal custom for a woman to be seen at such a time an exception had been made in the case of the *gaiour* woman who had come with Sakr-el-Droog.

Indeed, it would have taken more than Abd-el-Kadr to keep Gloria Ravissa away from the landing-platform at such a moment.

She was in the forefront gazing eagerly into the sky, while the speck that had been sighted by a look-out grew and grew in size until there could be no doubt about its identity.

The tribesmen set up a great shout as the 'plane swooped downwards and then banked steeply. But one voice did not join in. That silent voice was Gloria Ravissa's.

For she was puzzled. Where only one head showed above the rim of the cockpit there should have been three belonging to Brady, Liddle and Larida.

Abd-el-Kadr hadn't noticed this yet. With his men he was waving welcome to the return of Sakr-el-Droog. It was only when the Bat slid in gracefully and touched that he seemed to realise that the person in the machine was not the one he expected.

Gloria Ravissa had already recognised Rushton. His presence in the Bat without Brady was all she needed to tell her that some disaster had overtaken her partner.

Her hand dropped to the bag she clutched. For a moment she was tempted to draw her pearl-handled automatic and shoot Rushton as he climbed out. It would have been easy enough.

But she refrained. Here was the man who had last seen Brady, the only one through whom she could learn what had happened. If she killed him she might be completely cut off from Brady.

So she refrained and waited.

Reaching the ground, Grant Rushton stood erect and eyed the gathering. His gaze swept unnoticing past Gloria Ravissa. He was seeking the leader, and he picked out Abd-el-Kadr easily enough.

He had known the Riffians in the past. He had mixed much with the Arab races, and he knew the intricate but very necessary ceremony that must be gone through if insult were not to be taken.

He did his part gravely and patiently. When it was over he explained his purpose.

"I come from Sakr-el-Droog, noble sheik," he said solemnly. "It was impossible for him to return so soon as he promised. But his message to the *gaiour* woman is urgent, and I crave your permission to give it to her."

Abd-el-Kadr made a gesture of assent and courteously drew back, while Rushton beckoned Gloria Ravissa to come forward. She came, unwilling to obey his command, but knowing that she must.

Rushton took out the letter he had forced Brady to write, and handed it to her.

"Read that," he told her curtly, "and if you will take my advice, you will act upon it without delay."

She took it in silence and broke it open, she read.

Then she looked him in the eye.

"This says that I am to hand over to you certain money he left in my care."

"That is right—every peseta he got against those bonds."

"I could have killed you when you got out of that machine," she said savagely. "I wish I had."

"Then you never would have seen Brady again," he returned calmly. "I've taken good care, mademoiselle, that there shall be no hanky-panky in this business. And I would remind you that I am in a hurry. I wish to start on the return journey without delay. It is up to you to give Abd-el-Kadr the enclosed note which Brady has written to him. I believe he promises to return very soon."

"Will you take me to him?"

"I promised him I would do so on condition that the money and something else was handed over."

"I cannot refuse. But you may be sure we shall find some means of paying you off for this."

"Of course—of course," said Rushton wearily. "If you are coming, get busy, will you?"

And, hating him though she did, violently against her will though it was, she could do no other but obey.

When Grant Rushton and Tony took their final departure from Larida's *residencia,* it was to leave Brady and Liddle in charge of Gloria Ravissa, Larida and old Juan.

.   .   .   .   .

Since it would have been impossible in any event to secure bail for Mark Errol, Rushton did not press for it on his return to England.

Instead, he and Tony took up residence at Errol's house, and, during the wait for the trial, spent every possible moment in building up Rushton's theory into an iron-clad case that would withstand any legal or police torpedoing.

Not a word did Rushton say, even to Major Holden, about the high-powered .25 rifle which he had brought back from Spain, and which Brady had produced so reluctantly.

But at the rear of the premises of a certain gun-expert in London Rushton made certain tests, submitting the bullets afterwards to microscopic examination by one of the leading authorities.

Following that, he applied for and received police permission to have a similar test made of the bullet that had killed Carrie Richfield, the microscopic tests being photographed so that he could make comparison with those already in his possession.

Thus equipped, he waited with equanimity for the day of the trial, briefing for Errol's defence one of the first men at the Bar.

Rushton was, of course, the leading witness for the defence, but, from what had gone before he took the stand, it looked very bad for Errol. The police evidence had appeared devastating.

But the famous detective was as cool as ever as he stepped up and bowed to judge and jury. Then all eyes watched him as he smiled pleasantly at the prisoner and turned to face counsel.

The preliminaries were routine. But when counsel held up a small high-powered rifle of .25 calibre and began to question Rushton, not a sound but voices of counsel and witness could be heard in the court.

"You state that this is the rifle with which the crime was committed?"

"Yes."

"How did this rifle come into your possession?"

"I secured it in Spain a few days after the murder."

"From whom?"

"From the person who, in my belief, committed the crime."

"Can you give us his name?"

" 'Flash' Brady."

Sensation in court.

"And why are you so sure this was the weapon used?"

"I refer you to the reports of the experts."

There was a considerable time during which the photographs were handed to counsel, to the judge, and to the jury for examination.

Then adroitly counsel took Rushton along to tell of the other weapon, and why he was convinced, from the first, that the shot had not been fired from it.

From that point there could be no doubt of the result of the trial. When the question was finally put to the jury they returned a verdict without even leaving the box, and things were not made any sweeter for Inspector Blain when the judge publicly complimented Rushton upon the manner in which he had assembled his evidence and built up his case.

Rushton would have been less than human had he not been gratified at the final outcome of the affair.

Nevertheless, he was inwardly not completely satisfied. Nor would he be until he could see "Flash" Brady standing where Mark Errol had stood that day.

THE END.

[60000 WORDS]